THE
BURDEN
OF SECRETS

JILLIAN STORM

ISBN 978-0-578-63459-3

Published by:
Scribbles 'n Lit

This book is dedicated to all survivors
courageous enough to tell their stories.

~ J.S.

In all our lives, there is a fall from innocence.
A time after which we are never the same.

~ From the film *Stand by Me*

Contents

INTRODUCTION

Our house stood on McGillicutty Street. Like all houses in that part of Springdale, Connecticut, it stood cheek-to-jowl with the others. My favorite part of the street was its sounds— the summer sounds. Baseball bats thwacking in the street, the giggles from backyard hide and seek, the exultant shout after the successful capture of a firefly, the slap of wet sheets drying on back porch clotheslines, the welcoming tingle of the Good Humor truck as it crawled past our door, and the soft, soothing sighs of elms cooling the pavement.

Perry Como, Roy Orbison, and Steve and Edie crooned through open windows. Roller skates scraped against cement sidewalks, while baseball cards clickety-clicked between bicycle spokes. Hungry babies howled and mothers yelled at noisy children. Kids knew when to shout and when to whisper. Summer days were loud, lazy, laden with laughter.

The summer of 1962, I was 13. That's the summer I remember most—the summer I learned the burden of keeping secrets.

CHAPTER 1

June 19, 1962

My mother hummed as she went about her housework. It had been two years since she had seen her younger sister and finally, today was the day Aunt Addie was to arrive from Sacramento, California. I was probably more excited than Mom. My aunt's visits meant staying up late, playing cards at the dining room table, munching potato chips, drinking Coca-Cola, girl talk, and giggling—constant giggling from two sisters who shared a lifetime of stories and inside jokes. It would be two glorious weeks.

That June afternoon held anticipation. My father's blue Hudson zipped up the Merritt Parkway toward Bradley Airport. Dad was engrossed in Paul Harvey's news report, and I rode shotgun absorbed in my own thoughts. Mom had insisted on staying home with my seven-year-old twin brothers, Michael and Corey, while Dad and I were in charge of pick-up. Mom said she would stay behind to "freshen up the house for Addie," but I knew better. The house was fresh enough. It had been polished and re-polished for weeks. My mother's real reason was that she disapproved of my father's driving.

"Billy, don't drive like a cowboy late for the chuck wagon," she had warned, as she walked us to the car. My father rolled his eyes and nodded. "And Bibi, give these to my sister when she arrives." She laid a fresh-cut bouquet of white tea roses and bright red poppies in a cocoon of waxed paper and paper towels across my striped culottes.

I was enjoying the glow of being selected the female ambassador to greet my aunt at the airport, so I didn't notice the dark blue sedan with the flashing red lights burst onto the highway behind us, but my father did. He emitted a low groan and slapped the steering wheel as he slowed and pulled over onto the shoulder of the highway. I watched through the back window as the policeman got out of his car and slowly walked to the back of ours, wrote down our plate number, and then swaggered towards my father's open car window.

Dad switched off the radio and stared straight ahead, his jaw muscles clenching, the vein in his forehead pulsating. I stared straight ahead and listened to the exchange as my father, the cowboy was reined in.

"License and registration, sir."

Dad reached across me to the glove compartment and fumbled through candy wrappers and empty Pez dispensers before he found the car registration and passed it through the window. He bent forward and grabbed the wallet from his hip pocket and pulled out his license, handing over the tiny document that furnished entirely too much information as far as I was concerned— hair color, eyes, and exactly where we lived.

"How fast was I going, officer?" he grunted through clenched teeth.

"I clocked you at 72." The policeman took the documents and strode back to his car.

Dad slumped forward against the steering wheel and ran his hands through salt and pepper hair. "This'll cost me a month," he moaned.

I stared straight ahead, embarrassed for my father, as passing vehicles slowed to stare at us. A long, uncomfortable silence followed before he spoke. "Don't tell your mother, okay? I'll take care of it."

"Okay, Dad." *I sure didn't want to be the one to tell her.*

My thoughts raced. *Mom is right. He really does have a lead foot. Time to have a little fun with dear old Dad.* "Dad, is he going to drag you away in cuffs?" I straightened my jaw to keep from grinning when my father glared at me. "Is he going to send you up the river?"

"Bibi, you've been watching too many gangster movies. No, I'm not going 'up the river', but I'm probably going to lose my license for speeding. And your mother?" He winced and shook his head, "She's not going to be too happy about this."

I watched my father squirm as he waited. *Oh, this is too good! Should I stop needling him? Nah.* I remembered how he had teased me mercilessly last week when Teddy Kirk, who isn't even as old as me, had come to the door and asked if I wanted to go down to The Thunderbird to get an ice cream cone—his treat. I thought I'd die of embarrassment.

"If the cop takes your license away how will we get to the airport? I can't drive!"

"It'll be a while before they take it. I'll have to appear in court first."

I can't believe it. My father actually thinks I don't know that. I turned toward my window and ducked my head, allowing my hair to cascade into a dark side curtain shielding my face and my smirk. When I regained my composure, I turned toward him. "Court? Like on TV? I can see it all. An angry lawyer with dark, penetrating eyes," I raised my eyebrows and widened my eyes for effect. "He'll shake a meaty, accusatory finger at you." I waved my finger in front of him.

"Stop it," my father hissed.

I giggled. "A disapproving jury will glare at you as the prosecutor proclaims, 'Ladies and gentlemen, I implore you to do the right thing.'" I prayer-folded my hands in front of me as if pleading. "Mr. William Reilly stands before you guilty as charged. Guilty of driving like a cowboy. Lasso him and throw him into the county jail for thirty days with only stale bread and water."

"Okay, you can stop now."

I reached over and patted my father's hand. "But don't worry, Dad. Mom and I and the twins will visit every Sunday and smuggle heavy cakes filled with hack saw blades past the guards." I erupted in laughter.

He brushed my hand away. "Very funny!" He let out a low chuckle and shook his head. "I'll tell you one thing, kiddo, no one's going to laugh when your mother finds out about this."

I had to agree. My father and I sat waiting impatiently until the policeman returned to the car, handed my father back his license and registration and had him sign off on the ticket. Before leaving, the policeman lowered his head, peeked inside at me, shook a finger at my father and said, "Be a better role model for your young passenger."

As the policeman walked away, I gulped back a laugh and stared out the window. As I said, it was a time when kids knew when to shout and when to whisper. And this girl knew when to just plain shut up.

We drove away… slowly.

CHAPTER 2

Aunt Addie bounced off the Pan Am jet exactly on time. She looked more glamorous than ever. Her wavy auburn hair flowed to her shoulders and framed her perfectly made-up face. It was teased at the crown, making her look taller than the last time I had seen her. Silver droplets dangled and sparkled from pierced ears; while small oval sunglasses graced her freckled nose. I gave a dramatic curtsy and presented her with the bouquet before smothering her with kisses. She hugged me tight and curtsied in return to signal that our visit would be filled with secret girl codes and ceremonial gestures that only *we women* would understand.

"Bibi, I knew it. You're turning into a movie star. Look at you! You're a long-stemmed beauty! And look at that cute figure! You're getting curves in all the right places, girl. They're little now, but they're getting there." She patted my chest. "And it looks like you've got yourself a bra under that blouse!"

"Aunt Addie!" I rolled my eyes and cocked my head giving her "the look" that signaled her to stop talking about that stuff in front of my father.

Dad stepped closer. "Adeline, good to see you." He grinned and planted a chaste kiss on her cheek, then picked up the two largest pieces of her paisley luggage. I grabbed the third.

"Billy, you never change," my aunt chirped as she pinched his right cheek. "My sister's sure lucky to have such a handsome fox for a husband."

Dad blushed and grinned. Aunt Addie always had a way of disarming the biggest of giants.

We walked to the car and my aunt climbed into the back seat so she could "spread out for the ride." She oozed rose petals and oranges, a constant reminder to everyone around her of her thriving potpourri business back home, where she was known to all as the Herb Lady. But behind her back, Dad called her the Headache Lady. He couldn't stand her aroma for too long without getting a splitting headache. I was relieved when Aunt Addie climbed into the back seat. I remembered too well the last time she came to visit; I had taken the back seat coming home from the beach and threw up all over Corey's sweatshirt. The car smelled of vomit, really bad, so my aunt sprang into action and sprinkled lemon and lavender potpourri all over the seat and floor to absorb the stink. My father wasn't happy.

The next day he drove to Harry's Automotive and forked over fifteen dollars for the Super-Duper Gold Label Treatment. For weeks after, my father claimed he could still smell a faint scent of lemon and lavender. He said he would have been happier if she had simply left the puke.

On the ride home, my aunt regaled us with funny stories about my mother as a teenager and the recent antics of her house cats, Lily and Sassafrass, whom she had left behind under the watchful eyes of responsible neighbors. She spoke about the writers' group she now belonged to and her most recent letter to *The Sacramento Bee* in which she defended blocking the construction of a community bomb shelter in her neighborhood. "After all," she said. "If we're getting bombed, who wants to run like ninnies to a hole in the ground and spend time locked up with all those sweaty neighbors? I'd rather be outside where I can keep an eye on the devastation and use it as fodder for a writing project!"

"So cupcake, how are you spending your summer?" my aunt asked.

"Just hanging out with friends. 'Ya know, roller skating and stuff."

"She's actually pretty good at skating. She'll have to show you some of her twirls and crossover moves," Dad chimed in.

"That sounds like fun, sweetie. Before I go home, you'll have a performance for me?"

"Sure!"

The gentle lilt of my aunt's voice normally relaxed me, but all the way home I kept one eye on the speedometer and the other peeled for blue sedans with flashing lights.

No sooner had the car rolled to a stop in front of our house, than my aunt burst from the back seat and charged through the yard up our front steps and through the door. I looked at Dad and shrugged my shoulders. "I guess that means we get the bags again."

"You go along, Bibi. I'll take care of this," Dad said.

I didn't need to hear it a second time. I was a sucker for reunions, and I didn't want to miss one morsel of this one. I raced to the house to discover my mother and her little sister crushed in each other's arms, tears streaming down their faces, whispering as they held tight to each other. Michael and Corey stood by making goofy boy faces. I kept my distance and smiled as my mother and aunt had their "sister moment."

Dad wrestled my aunt's bags through the front door just as the women released each other. Mom dabbed her eyes and became all business. "Billy, you can put those bags up in Bibi's room. Addie will sleep in her bed." Mom turned to me. "I've set up the cot in there for you."

I could hardly contain myself. My aunt and I were going to be roomies!

"I'll take that, Dad." I grabbed the smallest bag and bounded up the stairs to my room to check out the setup. True to her word, my mother had set up the cot. It was close to the radiator. My rosebud comforter was draped across it, and gracing my aunt's bed was the white chenille bedspread reserved for sleepover guests. One of my grandmother's heart-shaped crocheted pillows had been placed at the head of the bed.

As I looked around the room, I envisioned my aunt and me sitting cross-legged on our assigned beds, chatting and telling funny stories, laughing about girl things into the wee hours of the night. I danced around the room and talked to my reflection in the mirror. "This is going to be cool!" I smiled and winked at myself and scampered downstairs.

Mom served pot roast that night. The conversation at the dinner table was more high-pitched than usual. Every time I looked over at my mother she was beaming, her cheeks flushed with excitement, intent on every word my aunt offered up. Dad was eager to interject humor through his Groucho Marx imitations. Aunt Addie got laughing so hard at "That's no lady. That's my wife," that she jumped up and danced around the room holding her crotch and had to race to the bathroom before she peed her pants. When my aunt was gone, my mom confided that laughing that hard was a trait that seemed to surface more often when the Treat sisters got together.

***

By the time Aunt Addie returned to the dinner table, Mom had already served up strawberry shortcake. The biscuits were warm and the whipped cream had started to form puddles on the plates. The table got quiet. I think it was partly because we were all savoring the dessert, and partly because we didn't want to get so silly again that my aunt would need to do another one of her dances.

Dad and I rose to clear the dishes. Michael and Corey raced into the living room to watch The Mickey Mouse Club, and the sisters lingered at the table over a bottle of Mateus rose´ my mother had purchased for my aunt's visit.

After we washed the dishes, Dad and I left the pots to soak and went our separate ways. My father found his chair and newspaper, and I made excuses to walk slowly by my mother and aunt a couple of times hoping to secure an invitation to join them. It didn't work and I started to feel a little foolish, so I sat down on the living room floor next to my brothers and watched the rest of their show with them. I thought Annette was beautiful, but I always wondered what she saw in that nerdy Bobby. Every now and then, I'd steal glimpses of my mother and aunt still seated at the table engrossed in conversation.

Except for the fact that they sported the same ski-jump, freckled noses and emitted the same high-pitched laugh, the sisters were as different as night and day.

My mother, ten years my aunt's senior, had shoulder-length straight chestnut hair with one natural streak of red that rose from the crown of her head and trailed down the back. Her pale blue eyes were large and piercing. She wore only a dab of pale rouge across both her cheeks and a touch of soft pink lipstick. She often remarked that a woman was only half dressed without her lipstick, so she applied hers frequently during the day. Mom's neat, white, Peter Pan-collared blouse was tucked into a pair of pink and green striped pedal pushers that were complemented by a pair of sensible Keds.

Aunt Addie, on the other hand, wore a V-neck, long-sleeved, ruffled, lime-green blouse that cascaded over a pair of bell-bottom blue jeans. A set of polished red toes peeked out from soft tan leather sandals. Green eyeshadow broke into tiny fans at her temples accentuating her hazel eyes. She liked to call it her "Avon come-hither look."

The TV show ended, and Dad turned on the news while I shepherded my brothers upstairs to supervise baths and get them into their pajamas. When they were settled in their room with Lincoln logs and GI Joes, I grabbed my favorite book and wandered back downstairs. *Watch for a Tall White Sail* was about a young woman who was pining for her love to return from sea and it was the first romance novel I had ever read. Usually, I was captivated by it, but I couldn't concentrate tonight. I kept sneaking glances over at the twosome in the dining room. It was times like this I wished I had a sister of my own.

Okay, they've had enough time alone. I'm going in. I strolled into the dining room and plopped myself down next to my aunt. I was just getting into the conversation when the mantle clock above the fireplace delivered eight smooth beats.

My mother straightened. "Bibi, it's eight o'clock. Would you tuck your brothers in for me? And make sure they say their prayers."

I couldn't believe she was asking me to do this. I stomped up the stairs. *Enough is enough. Mom should be saying prayers with the boys and getting them one more drink of water. Why do I have to do all the dirty work? When do I get any time with my aunt?*

***

When I came back downstairs, my mother and aunt were speaking in hushed tones, so I knew better than to interrupt that. I stole looks at them from behind my book and tried to read their lips. Whatever they were saying seemed pretty juicy.

Dad had turned on the Yankees game, and I was definitely feeling like the outsider. I couldn't stand it. I had to think of something. *Hmmm. Yes, that might work. I may be an outsider, but I'm an outsider with a plan.*

I sauntered across the room and sat on the arm of my father's chair. "Dad, when are you going to tell Mom about you-know-what?" I spoke in a stage whisper.

He scowled and whispered, "Later."

"I really think she needs to be told." I gave him my most stern look.

"I said I'll get to it later. Now's not the right time."

"What are you two whispering about?" my mother's voice sounded from the dining room. I looked up and she and my aunt were looking our way. My mother had an uncanny knack for zeroing in on every activity around her, while still able to hold up her part of a conversation. That annoying habit of hers was just what I was betting on to activate my plan.

"Oh, nothing!" I answered in a sing-song, overly dramatic fashion, which could only signal we were definitely talking about something. And she had better get to the bottom of it. I scooted back over to the couch, picked up my book, and pretended to read.

I felt my mother's keen eyes studying my father and me. "Billy?'

"Mary, I'll talk to you later," he said, his gaze returning to the TV.

My mother went back to her conversation, but she seemed a little distracted. Yes. I'd planted the seed.

A couple of minutes later my mother whispered something to my aunt, and Aunt Addie stood up, poured herself another glass of wine to take with her, and asked me if I'd like to help her unpack her things and find some room in my closet. Would I! I clambered up the stairs after her, making sure not to meet my father's eyes as I passed him.

I followed Aunt Addie into my bedroom and closed the door behind us. After all, I was sure my parents would need some privacy. Boy, *would* they need some privacy. I felt like a traitor, but desperate times...desperate measures. Now I had my aunt all to myself.

Aunt Addie set her electric curlers on the edge of the vanity. She passed me a couple of dresses and a gorgeous blue silk blouse to hang in the closet. I emptied two drawers for her extra clothes. When her bags were almost empty, she pulled out a yummy orange flowered pair of pedal pushers and a matching midriff top and handed them to me. "For you," she said.

"For me?" I squealed. I ran over to the mirror and held the outfit up in front of me. I whipped off my culottes and blouse and tried on the new outfit. I was transformed. The new pants hugged my legs and bottom. At first, I folded my arms across my bare middle, feeling a little self-conscious. With my aunt inspecting me, I stared at myself in the mirror. I looked like a real teenager.

"Stand up straight and put your hands down by your side. I want to get the full effect," chided my aunt.

I stared at myself and giggled twirling around and checking the outfit from the rear, then again from the front. "Do you think my mother is actually going to let me wear this?"

"Why not? So it shows a little skin. You've got the figure for it. It's summertime, girl!"

"Yeah, it's summertime!" I grinned. I wanted to run downstairs to model my new look for my parents, but by the sounds of it, they were occupied. Angry voices drifted upstairs. Pots and pans banged, and then banged some more.

"So, young lady, what's going on down there? And don't say 'Nothing.' This is your godmother you're talking to."

I felt my face grow hot and I put my head down.

"Bibi, I know you masterminded this little scene downstairs tonight, and I want to know what you know."

I didn't reply. My aunt waited.

"Bibi?"

"When we were on our way to the airport, Dad got pulled over for speeding. He thinks he'll lose his license." As soon as it was out, I felt like a tattletale.

"Oh." My aunt didn't say anything for a few seconds. "How fast was he going?"

"72."

"Whoa!" Her eyebrows shot up. She blew air out between her teeth and took a long sip of her wine.

Without missing a beat, my aunt reached for one of my record albums. "Connie Francis! I love her!" She slid the cover off and turned on the record player. As soon as she placed the needle on the vinyl disk, Connie's sultry voice drowned out the commotion downstairs. My aunt and I sat side by side on the low vanity bench in front of the mirror, and put on our best pouty lips. I grabbed two hairbrushes and handed her one to use for a microphone. Yes, this is what I had dreamed of. Fun times like this. My aunt… my own pretend big sister. As we lip-synched the lyrics to "Who's Sorry Now?" I couldn't help but think of my father doing battle downstairs and the long summer he had ahead of him. I snuggled closer to my aunt and smiled at our reflection.

And then I cranked up the volume.

CHAPTER 3

I awoke early the next morning with an uneasy feeling in my stomach. My father's face came to mind, and I immediately felt remorse for causing the previous night's nasty scene. I looked over at my aunt's bed, but only a lump of covers remained. Although the bed had been slept in, she was no longer in it. A slight moan and shuffling came from down the hall and the toilet flushed. I heard the moan again and followed the sounds to the bathroom. I tapped on the bathroom door. "Aunt Addie? Is everything okay?"

"Uh, yeah. I'll be right out."

I heard a heave and the unmistakable sound of vomiting from the other side of the door.

"'Ya want me to get Mom?"

"No, don't bother your mother. I'll be right out."

I waited on the other side of the door as she flushed again and then started to brush her teeth. A few minutes later, the door opened. Morning sunlight streamed through her nightgown offering a silhouette of large breasts and a narrow waist. My aunt's face was the color of classroom paste, her eyes watery.

She stumbled out into the hall. I eyed her up and down. "You all right?"

"Yes. I guess something didn't agree with me from last night's dinner." She gave a wan smile. "I'm going back to bed for a little while." She lumbered past me and headed for the bedroom. "Still on California time."

"Are you sure you don't want me to get Mom? She might have some Bromo Seltzer."

"I'm sure. I'll be fine, really. Don't bother your mother."

I followed her back to the bedroom and snuggled in under the covers with her. "I'll rub your back. Maybe that will relax you like it does Mom when she's sick."

"That would be lovely, sweetheart. Thank you." She wriggled further down under the covers. Before long, I heard the slow in and out of my aunt's breathing. I drifted off next to her, making my plans for the day.

My brothers woke up at about 8:30 and brought the house to attention.

I got up and headed downstairs. The smell of Saturday morning bacon wafted through the air. As my father walked by me, he swatted me across the rear with the rolled-up morning paper.

"Hey! What was that for?"

He glared at me. "I just wanted to add a little more excitement around here. I know how much you like excitement."

I felt my face redden, and I lowered my eyes. "Sorry."

"Next time someone tells you to keep a secret, keep your mouth shut. I wanted to tell your mother when the time was right."

"And the time wasn't right?"

My father sighed. "What do you think?"

I gave him a weak smile. "I guess not."

My mother stood in front of the iron skillet frying bacon. When I walked into the kitchen, she looked up. "Well, look who it is." She scowled. "Is there anything you need to inform me of today, young lady? Out with it, if you do."

"No, nothing yet." I rolled my eyes. Actually, I was sort of relieved my mother knew about my father's ticket, but still, I was ashamed of myself for hatching such an underhanded plot. "Sorry, Mom."

"You can get back on my good side by cracking eight of those eggs in this bowl." She handed me the orange plastic mixing bowl. "Is your aunt awake yet?"

"Nope. She got up earlier and wasn't feeling well, so she went back to bed."

"She's sick?"

"Who's sick?" I turned at my aunt's voice. She stood in the kitchen doorway wrapped in a silk blue robe, her hair smoothed and a glow on her freshly-washed face. "Nothing that a piece of toast and some of that delicious-smelling bacon won't cure. I'm starved."

"Oh, I forgot. You don't eat eggs." Mom turned to me. "Crack only six eggs. The boys will have cereal."

My aunt reached for a cup and saucer and poured herself coffee.

My mother turned the bacon. "I'm sorry I gave you the bum's rush last night, Addie. Billy and I had something to discuss, and it took a little longer than I thought it would."

"I guess it would." She cocked her head to the side. "Miss Priss told me all about it."

"She did, did she?" Mom glared at me.

I turned away and started to whisk the eggs as vigorously as I could.

"Mary, I pried it out of her. After all, your "discussion" was pretty hard to ignore. And a speeding ticket is not the end of the world."

"It's not the end of *your* world. You're here for a couple of weeks and then go back to your glamorous life. I'm the one stuck chauffeuring everyone around—the one who has to endure the neighbors' looks. This neighborhood thrives on gossip like this."

"Mary, you're too concerned about what others think. You always were. Tell them all to go to hell."

"Addie!" My mother looked in my direction.

"Oh, don't get your liver in a quiver! Bibi's a teenager, for heaven's sake. I think she's heard the expression before."

"Not around here, she hasn't. So put a lid on it."

Aunt Addie winked at me. "Sorry, cupcake."

I smiled back.

"Okay, let's get this show on the road," my aunt said. "Just point me toward the bread and the toaster, and I'll make myself useful."

Fifteen minutes later, everyone was seated at the breakfast table planning our first day together. Dad would take the twins for haircuts and to the park to throw some balls around; the girls would shop for the annual neighborhood summer solstice party planned for the next day. As long as I could remember, my parents had hosted the picnic in our backyard. The neighbors looked forward to it as much as we did as the first official rite of summer.

Two hours later, my mother, my aunt, and I walked a couple of blocks to Bongo's Department Store. We quickly gathered streamers, paper lanterns, and other paper goods. It was a quiet day at the store; most would-be customers were home in front of a fan or initiating the summer with a dip in the town pool.

Before too long we had everything we needed and hustled to the checkout.

Mom introduced Aunt Addie to old Mr. Cortini, the store clerk, and we stood by as my aunt flirted her way to a five percent discount. After all, she "had come all the way from Sacramento to shop for Bongo bargains." Before she left, Aunt Addie tossed a smile and a wink to old Mr. Cortini who insisted, "Please call me George, Adeline. As a matter of fact, please call me anything except late for dinner." He snorted and broke into fits of hog laughter.

Aunt Addie responded with a coquettish little, "Oh George, you rascal."

As soon as we got out of the store, the three of us exploded into laughter, my mother fluttering her eyelashes and reenacting the flirting scene on the walk home. I chimed in taking the part of please-call-me-George in my finest baritone voice. Each time I did it, my aunt and mother howled. We kept up the teasing and silliness until my aunt pleaded with us, on behalf of her bladder and her dignity, to stop.

When we arrived home Mom offered to make some lemonade, and I unpacked the shopping bags. Aunt Addie scampered upstairs to fix her smudged mascara.

After I unpacked the bags and gulped some lemonade, I headed up to the attic for the large cardboard smiling sun and moon that would complete our solstice party decorations. As I passed my bedroom, I spotted my aunt hunched over her makeup case. I tiptoed up behind her and saw she had removed the top compartment of the makeup case and was holding a clear bottle of liquid to her lips. "Freshening your breath, my dear?" I said in my deepest please-call-me-George voice. My aunt jumped and whipped the bottle behind her back.

"What's the matter with you, sneaking up on me like that!" she glared at me through raccoon eyes.

"I-I-I was just kidding."

"Well, next time, knock."

I ran out of the room up the short flight of steps to the safety of the attic. My heart raced as I fought back tears. *I was only kidding. This is what Mom* always *warns me about—crossing the line. "Bibi, you always overdo. You always take it too far. Enough is enough!"*

I sat with my head in my hands.

The attic was dark and musty. A perfect place to hide humiliation. My aunt's words roared through my head. "What's the matter with you?" *What is the matter with me?* Hot tears dripped down my cheeks. *How long can I hide up here before they start to look for me? Should I just turn myself in to my mother? Risk upsetting her again? Maybe I'll escape across the street and hide out at the Kennedys' house for a couple of hours. Darlene will know what to do. If I give Aunt Addie time alone, maybe she'll forget what an idiot I am.*

Just as I had decided on my escape plan, the attic door squeaked open and delivered a narrow gleam of daylight. My aunt stood in the doorway. "Bibi, are you in here?"

I didn't move.

"Come on, I know you're in here, cupcake." My aunt turned on the light and came toward me. I shielded my eyes and looked at the floor so she couldn't see me sniffling like a baby.

She came over and knelt in front of me. "I'm sorry, honey. I didn't mean to growl at you. Your aunt's getting persnickety in her old age."

I looked up, and a warm tear dripped down the side of my nose. I brushed it away and sniffed back the snot that was on the verge of leaking down my lip any second. My aunt looked normal again. Her mascara was fixed, her green eye fans back in place, and her hot-pink lipstick professionally applied—a walking Avon commercial. I put my arm around her waist. "I'm sorry. I should have knocked. I know it's not just my room anymore. I'm not used to sharing it with anyone."

"It *is* your room, sweetie. It's just that I didn't expect George Cortini to follow me home."

I giggled.

"Your imitation was spot on, you know. You just caught me and my bottle of mouthwash off guard, that's all. Let's forget about it, okay? It'll be our little secret. Deal?"

"Deal." I looked up into my aunt's beautiful face and felt my body relax. "You're the coolest aunt ever and no way am I going to wreck *this* secret." I picked up the cardboard sun and moon, and we turned out the attic light on our way back downstairs.

By evening, things even seemed back to normal, and this time when Mom and Aunt Addie lingered at the supper table over a glass of wine, I did the dishes and made myself scarce.

CHAPTER 4

I awoke to the long rumble of thunder. My aunt stood in front of my open bedroom window looking out onto the street. She held a glass in her hand. A whoosh of warm air sent the sheer curtains swirling around her body. I wanted to be sure not to startle her again, so I whispered, "Aunt Addie?"

"Are you awake?" she whispered back.

"Uh huh. It feels like it's getting ready to rain."

"Yeah, I think we're in for a good one. I can never sleep during a storm. I feel as if I'm missing out on something."

"Me too," I said, wiping the sleep from my eyes and glancing over at my glow-in-the-dark clock. It read 2:30 A.M.

"Did your mother ever tell you what we used to do during thunderstorms?"

"I don't think so," I said.

"We used beach towels, spread them out, and sat on them pretending they were magic carpets. As the wind roared, our carpets carried us to any exotic place we wanted to go. Your mother and I created some fantastic stories that way. Mine were always better, but don't tell her I told you that," she chuckled.

"I won't." I tore off my covers. "Will these do?" I asked as I turned on the bedroom light and drew two colorful beach towels from my tote bag.

"They'll do just fine."

I started to lay them out on the floor in front of the window. My aunt stopped me. "No, you don't understand. We did this *outside*."

"No way! Mom would never do that in a thunderstorm. It's too dangerous."

"Your mother? Think it's too dangerous? Ha! Who do you think taught me?"

My aunt put her glass on the dresser, grabbed a towel, and started out the bedroom door before I had a chance for that statement to sink in. It didn't take me more than a New York minute to follow her lead.

When I got to the backyard, my aunt was already getting situated on her magic carpet. My eyes adjusted to the darkness, and I could see her legs were crossed in front of her, her head and shoulders thrown back facing the sky as if daring the storm to begin. I spread out my towel next to her and mimicked her position.

As the wind built, trees swayed and bent, readying themselves for the action. The earthy scent of approaching rain grew stronger. Two bolts of lightning illuminated the night sky. A grumble of thunder followed.

"Mon ami, je suis Américaine," my aunt began. "It's delightful in Paris, n'est pas? The fashions are exquisite. Look at that lovely feathered hat and that pencil skirt mademoiselle is wearing. You won't see that back in the States."

My aunt, the world traveler.

Plop...plop. The first fat raindrops fell onto my cheeks. I stole a look over at my aunt and saw she was smiling as drop after drop dripped down her cheeks onto her nightgown. The rain came faster now.

"Oklahoma, where the wind comes whippin' down the plain!" I sang out and giggled. "Howdy partner. You're lookin' fine in your fancy buckskin and rattlesnake boots. Hold onto that hat or it'll blow away. Keep that pistol in its holster. Don't want it to get wet or it's likely to rust."

"You're getting it," my aunt said. "Go on, you're doing fine."

I needed a moment to bask in my aunt's praise and get back into character. As I paused to think of something else clever enough to warrant more praise, the back-porch light came on, and lit up the backyard.

"Addie! Bibi! What in the world are you two doing out here?" My mother stood on the back porch.

Uh, oh. I'm in for it now.

"As soon as the two of you think the rest of the house is asleep, you come sneaking out here in the middle of the night and...and...you don't even ask me to join you?"

My mother whipped out a beach towel from behind her back and danced through the rain. I couldn't believe what I was seeing. She plopped down, crossed her legs, threw back her shoulders, and began. "Bona sera, signore. Yes, a large scoop of lemon gelato would be fine. I am strolling through the streets of Siena..."

The three of us sat side by side, telling stories revealing our personal flights of fancy, each of us trying to outshine the other. Three fearless women in pajamas, wet heads dripping, goddesses of nature, experiencing the most magical rides of our lives.

A giant crack of lightning sent my mother and me running toward the house.

"Where are you two scaredy babies going? A little rain isn't going to hurt you! Come back! Come back now!" my aunt screamed at the top of her lungs.

My mother and I stopped when we reached the safety of the small awning over the back porch. Aunt Addie sat glued to her sopping towel riding out the storm. She clutched her knees to her chest and rocked back and forth, her head thrown back, letting the rain drip down her hair and through her nightgown.

"Get in out of the rain, you ninny. You'll get electrocuted!" shouted my mother.

"I'm staying right here and riding it out. This is the best storm I've been in in years, and I'm not letting my 'fraidy pants' big sister ruin it for me like she always did before."

"Oh yeah? Well, when you get electrocuted, don't expect me to claim the body!" my mother yelled back. "I'll just leave you there in that drippy wet nightgown and use you as a yard ornament."

"And I'll be the best-looking yard ornament you'll ever have!"

My mother burst out laughing and shook her head. She turned to me. "Come on. Let's get inside. We're as wet as a Sicilian grandmother's tear ducts."

I scampered up the steps and into the mudroom. While I was drying off, I peeked out the window at my aunt. "I can't believe she's still out there. When do you think she'll come in?"

"When she thinks she's made her point that she's braver and wilder than I'll ever be."

I looked over at my mother. "She is, you know." I peered through the window at my aunt and grinned.

My mother chuckled. "Well, maybe she's wilder…maybe she's even braver… but I'm smarter." She gave a twisted smile and wiggled her eyebrows to signal she was up to no good.

Then my mother reached over, flicked off the backyard light, and locked the door.

"Wait! What about Aunt Addie?"

My mother delivered a smug smile. "I told you. *I'm* smarter."

CHAPTER 5

The next day dawned sunny and warm, a perfect beginning to the day of our summer solstice party. When we were all in the kitchen, Dad teased my aunt about having to unlock the door for a "certain someone who didn't have enough sense to come in out of the rain." Mom feigned surprise and carried a smug smirk all the way through breakfast.

After breakfast, Mom was all business as she rallied the troops to decorate our three-bay garage. Out came the three folding tables for the buffet. Around noon, John Caldwell delivered and set up a canopy and thirty folding chairs, a contribution every year from his funeral home. The women were in charge of streamers, lanterns, and hanging the moon and sun.

Dad was in charge of the most exotic of the decorations. He hammered in five Hawaiian torches on either side of the stone pathway that wound through the yard. Michael and Corey kept busy coloring paper placemats to scatter over yellow plastic tablecloths. By 1 o'clock the backyard looked like party city. I looked forward to dusk when my father would ignite the torches, and the yard would fill with neighbors bearing smiles and all kinds of savory foods.

Satisfied that the decorating was finished, Mom and my aunt headed back to the kitchen to prepare lunch and take a breather. I took this time to sneak up to my room and change into the new outfit Aunt Addie had given me.

As I admired my reflection in the mirror, I heard my brothers and the rest of the neighborhood boys playing baseball in the street. Someone yelled, "Car!" I looked out the window and watched a red Pontiac Bonneville pull up in front of the Polanskys' house. My girlfriend Nancy's twenty-two-year-old cousin, Stanley, home on leave from the service, was arriving for his yearly visit. My friends and I drooled over him when he sported his military khakis. Every summer he grew cuter and cuter.

My heart did a quick somersault as I watched him hop out of his car and walk around to the trunk. *This is perfect timing. I'll just pretend I'm going over to see what Nancy is up to.*

I bolted down the steps and out the front door, practically vaulting over two front lawns to the Polanskys' house. I stopped just short of Stanley's car and slowed to my most practiced teenage stroll as he yanked a brown suitcase out of the trunk, his uniform shirt clinging to well-defined biceps. "Oh, hi Stanley!" I tried to sound casual.

"Hi." He flashed a broad smile as he slammed the trunk and looked me up and down. His gaze stopped at my bare midriff. I folded my arms and hunched over a little to cover my stomach. *Maybe this wasn't such a good idea after all.* "Dee Dee isn't it?"

"It's Bibi."

"Close, but no cigar, huh?" He placed his suitcase at his feet and dug into his chest pocket for a pack of Lucky Strike cigarettes. He tapped one out of the package and reached into his pants pocket for some matches. "Care for one?"

"Uh, no thanks. I don't smoke...yet." I smiled. *I can't believe he thinks I'm old enough to smoke. This outfit is working better than I thought.* I relaxed and straightened. "So, I see you have a suitcase. Are you spending the night?"

"More than a night. I'm on leave for a month, and it feels great."

My heart raced. *A whole month! Yes!* "So, you'll be coming to our summer solstice party tonight? Nancy and your aunt and uncle are coming."

"Only if you're going to be there looking as flirty as you do now." His azure eyes twinkled and slowly inventoried every inch of me.

I felt my face redden and my stomach muscles tighten. "It's at my house! Of course, I'm going to be there, silly." I gave him my widest grin and drew my arms behind my back so he could stare as much as he wanted. *That's it. Give him a real eyeful.*

"And what *you're* wearing is absolutely fine with me." I returned the wink. *Look at me! I'm a flirt*!

"Well, I guess I better get in there." He cocked his blond crewcut in the direction of Nancy's house. Are you coming, too?"

That's right. I was supposed to be visiting Nancy. "You know, I forgot I had to do something. Tell Nancy I'll see her tonight. Bye, Stan." Stan sounded much more mature than Stanley. I turned and sauntered down the sidewalk to my house.

"Bye, sexy. See ya later!" he shouted to me from Nancy's doorstep. *Did he just call me "sexy" in front of the whole neighborhood?* I shot a glance over at my brothers praying they hadn't heard him. Nope. Still engrossed in their game. *Sexy! I'm sexy! Twenty-two-year-old Stan thinks I'm sexy!*

As soon as I saw that "Mr. Movie Star" was inside Nancy's house, I broke into a sprint, past the boys and up through my front door where I stopped short when I came face to face with my mother. Her eyes grew wide and her jaw dropped as she eyed me from head to toe. "W-w-what? Barbara Ann? What are you wearing? Where are you coming from?"

I could tell my new orange outfit wasn't having the same effect on my mother as it had on Stan. Mom only used my full name when she was annoyed.

"Um…I was over Nancy's."

"Where did you get that outfit?"

"I, uh…"

"Oh, no! Addie!"

"Mom, Aunt Addie brought this all the way from California for me. I love it. It makes me look grown up." My mind raced for the words I needed to convince my mother to let me wear the outfit that night. After all, Stan was counting on it. "You need to let me show a little skin. It's summertime." I decided to quote my aunt. Bad move.

My mother's eyebrows shot up and her pretty faced turned into an angry, ugly scowl. "You march up to your room and put on a decent blouse, young lady. Now!" My mother tore out of the living room. I knew I wasn't the only one who had to face her wrath.

I stomped up the stairs and plopped myself down on the bed. *I'm not her little girl anymore. I'm sexy. Stan said so, and my mother's too old-fashioned or jealous to realize it. That's it. My own mother is jealous of me. I'm prettier. If I wore outfits like this all the time, I'd always be prettier, and she can't stand the thought of that. I'll sneak out if I have to. I'll save all my allowance and send it off to Aunt Addie. I'll have her buy me one of these outfits in pink and blue and green and…whew, this room smells. What is that odor?*

I opened the window. Outside, angry voices rose from the backyard. I heard my mother's voice. "…my daughter…growing up quick enough!"

And then my aunt's voice. "Can't coddle her forever…I don't understand why…"

Go, Aunt Addie. I'm on your side. My mother has to let me grow up some day.

As I listened to my mother and aunt arguing, my anger faded and I felt a strange uneasiness and guilt wash over me. Those two always got along. I had never heard them exchange cross words before. *First, my mother and father fighting—now this. What have I done?*

I closed the window and removed the orange top, carefully placing it in my bottom drawer. From my closet, I selected my white sleeveless peasant blouse and tucked it into my pants. I looked in the mirror and decided I looked like me again. My pants were still cool. A half-sexy outfit was better than none.

Boy, this room stinks. What is that smell? I peeked in the wastebasket. There were only a few tissues with lipstick blots on them and my aunt's empty bottle of mouthwash covered with clumps of potpourri. I lifted the empty bottle. The pungent smell assaulted my nose. *What kind of mouthwash is this?* The label was missing. I walked down the hall to the linen closet and retrieved a brown paper bag in which to dump the garbage. When I opened the window again to air out the room, all was quiet in the backyard.

Creeping down the stairs, I headed for the garbage. Mom and Aunt Addie had come inside and were working quietly in the kitchen stuffing tuna and egg salad tea sandwiches. As I passed through the kitchen my mother looked up, gave me the once-over, and muttered, "That's more like it."

Aunt Addie shrugged her shoulders and offered a weak smile.

"After I dump this trash, I'm going over to Darlene's house to see what she's doing. Okay?"

My mother nodded. "Tell Marla I'll see her tonight. Can't wait for some of her pineapple upside-down cake. Oh, and before you go to Darlene's take this invitation up the hill and stick it in Mrs. Brown's mailbox. I want to make sure she knows about the party. Maybe she'll surprise us and attend this year."

"Old Lady Brown? She never goes out for anything. Besides, Jimmy Springer says he saw her once standing near her barn door holding a rifle."

"First of, she's Mrs. Brown to you, young lady. And I don't have much confidence in anything that comes out of Jimmy Springer's mouth. Here." She slapped the invitation into my hand. "When your father and I moved into this house, Edna and George Brown were very kind to us. Now that George is gone, she needs invitations like this to assure her that she's still a part of this neighborhood. Now scoot."

I heaved a long sigh and then hustled out to the garbage cans with my bag of garbage. As I opened the lid, there lay a copy of the previous night's *Stamford Advocate*. The front page featured a smiling girl about my age. The headline above the picture read "Police Investigate another Missing Girl." The article went on... "Barbara Harrington, 13, last seen on Grove Street...the fourth missing teenager since April...blue blouse, brown shorts, hair ribbon with her name stitched into it...rapist...serial killer..." The story sent a chill through me. I stuffed the newspaper with the dead girl's picture back down into the bin and squished my bag of garbage on top of it.

I raced up the hill to Mrs. Brown's house and quickly deposited the invitation in her mailbox, stole a fleeting glance at her tired-looking barn, then shot down the street to the Kennedys' house.

Darlene and her mother were just finishing up baking the cake and the house smelled like a high-class bakery. "My mom said to tell you that she's really looking forward to that cake, Mrs. Kennedy."

"I put extra pineapple on it for her." She smiled. "And extra cherries for your brothers."

Darlene and I slipped upstairs to her room. I filled her in on every detail of my day from wearing the new outfit, to Nancy's dreamy cousin being in town for a whole month, to my mother's anger. I left out the sexy part though, because frankly, my best friend was known for her very big mouth. I decided that detail would be something only Stan and I would share. I did tell her about the serial killer, though. It was pretty satisfying to see Darlene's big brown eyes grow wide as I told her what I had read. She was never easy to impress.

Darlene seemed as excited to see Stan as I was. "Bibi, help me pick out something flashy to wear tonight if Stan's going to be there." She whipped her hands through her thick, dark locks and smiled at me with straight, perfect teeth.

Ugh! Whenever I helped Darlene pick through her closet it turned into a Hollywood production in every sense of the word—a production starring Darlene who insisted on parading back and forth on the long runner rug in front of her full-length mirror, throwing her hips one way and then the other while I stood to the side narrating and describing every outfit the *lovely* Darlene was modeling.

By the time she finally settled on her green-flowered blouse and her white clam diggers and I had talked her into letting me borrow her favorite gold heart-shaped locket to jazz up my outfit, it was time for me to go home and get ready to greet the neighbors.

A half hour later, I was at the end of my driveway awaiting our guests, role-playing memorable ways to greet a "certain soldier." *Stan, so nice to see you again... Well, look who the cat dragged in... Welcome to your first summer solstice party (I could gently take his arm). I'm Bibi and I will be your hostess for the evening.... Or maybe I'll just break into song "Soldier boy, oh my little soldier boy, I'll get punch for you."*

The first to arrive were the Murphys. Mrs. Murphy hugged me. She smelled of Jean Nate lotion and deviled eggs. Donna and Gary followed behind, each carrying a bag of chips. They bolted straight into the backyard searching for Michael and Corey. "Danny will come by later after his baseball game," Mrs. Murphy reported. "I know he doesn't want to miss the party and all the young people." She winked at me and I felt my face flush.

Next, came the Kennedys with their upside-down cake. Darlene looked great in the outfit we had picked out earlier. She had teased her hair a little and applied her pink-ice lipstick. She wanted to greet people with me, but her parents insisted she come with them and say hello to my parents first. As soon as she left, I pinched my cheeks and bit my lips to give them a little more color.

Down the sidewalk marched Nancy and her parents and the kielbasa. No Stan. I greeted them and they offered that Stan had decided to take a quick shower, so he'd be over later. Nancy made a beeline for Darlene. The Petersons and the O'Learys came down the street with their gangs. Old Mr. and Mrs. Fillmore arrived from up the block. Mrs. Fillmore brought one of her heavy chocolate cakes with no frosting that required a gallon of milk to swallow a piece.

As I escaped from old man Fillmore's cigar-smelling bear hug, I spotted Stan gliding down the driveway. He looked as good in civilian clothes as he did in uniform. He had changed into a pair of Wranglers and a tie-dyed tee shirt that clung to his muscular chest. I completely forgot anything I had practiced.

"Hi flirt," he said.

"Hi." I swallowed.

"If you're the official welcoming committee, I sure feel welcomed." He grinned as he looked me over. I felt my stomach flip flop and my legs start to quiver.

Before I knew what was happening, he flicked my hair back and laid a soft hand on my neck. He tugged ever so gently on the elastic in my peasant blouse, nudging it slightly to expose my right shoulder. Then he did the same to the other side. "There. That's the way that blouse should be worn. It shows off your beautiful tan and that special locket." He picked the heart locket up off my neck and held it between his fingers for a long moment as I melted into his eyes. "I hope the guy who gave you this knows how lucky he is."

Oh, no! He thinks there's someone else! "There's no other guy, Stan. Really. I borrowed it from Darlene for the night. Her father gave it to her for her birthday."

"Well, that's a relief. I thought I had competition. Now why don't you introduce me around, sexy. I want to meet all the neighbors."

As I turned to walk toward the party, Stan ran a soft finger across my left shoulder down my back and stopped at the top of my backside. "Hey!" I jumped a bit at the unexpected gesture and instinctively elbowed him.

"Oh, sorry. I didn't mean…." He cast his eyes downward. "I forgot for a second," he stammered. "Oh, man. Maybe I should just go back to my aunt and uncle's." He turned to leave.

Oh no! He can't leave! "No, Stan. It's okay. You just…uh… didn't realize, that's all. Please stay. For me?" I touched his arm. "Come on, I'll introduce you around, and we'll forget it happened. Anyone can make a mistake, right?"

He smiled at me and I melted for the second time in five minutes. "Wow. You're great. Every girl should be as understanding as you. Okay, you win. We'll forget it ever happened, all right? No one has to know but you and me. Our secret."

"Sure, just you and me," I shot back.

"Ah, that's my girl."

His girl? He just called me his girl!

"I think I hear a party happening. Why don't you introduce me to all your friends?" He turned and walked in the direction of the party. I floated in beside him.

I poured a glass of punch for Stan and started introducing him around. Uncle Greg learned he was home on leave and held him captive with stories from his own service in the National Guard and how he had no respect for draft dodgers. Dad came along and joined us. He took one look at my blouse and pulled it up onto my shoulders. "There you go. I think that's the way it's supposed to look. Now you're perfect."

I looked Stan's way and rolled my eyes.

"Bibi, I think your mother was looking for you earlier," said Dad. I took that as my cue to get lost and leave them alone to their guy talk.

I sought out my mother who put me in charge of making plates of food for Mr. and Mrs. Fillmore. As soon as I could, I escaped to find Darlene and Nancy. They were standing apart from the other guests. Darlene was riddling Nancy with questions about Stan. By the time I arrived, Detective Darlene was ready to report.

"Bibi, do you know Stan spends his leave with Nancy's family every year because his parents both died in a car crash a few years ago? He doesn't have a regular girlfriend, at least not one that Nancy has ever met. He loves hot rods and golf and attended Worcester Art School before he went into the service. I think that's where my cousin, Ernie, goes to school. I know all about art school." Darlene glowed with importance as she delivered each morsel of information. I listened and absorbed all the facts and mentally filed them away. They would make good conversation items when I found myself alone again with Stan.

Speaking of Stan, I glanced over to where I had left him. Miraculously, he had escaped from Uncle Greg and my father. But where was he? I looked around and noticed him at the food table loading up his plate. My aunt stood next to him acting her usual goofy self. She held a stalk of celery between her teeth and a rose in her hair. Al Martino's rich voice belted out "Volare," and she danced around Stan like some sort of a Spanish temptress.

I walked over to the table. "Ready to enter your world of make-believe, Aunt Addie?" I chuckled.

"Señorita, please move out of my way while I entertain this gringo." My aunt danced over to me and threw her hip into my side, nudging me aside. I looked at Stan who was grinning from ear-to-ear, his eyes moving from my aunt to me, back to my aunt. She started to clap her hands and stomp her feet as if she was a toreador fighting a bull. I burst out laughing at the sight of my aunt, the show-off. Then Stan started to laugh.

Darlene and Nancy ran over to see what all the commotion was, and Darlene mimicked my aunt's dance steps and got into the act. Stan started taking on the role of another bull fighter and moved around Darlene and Aunt Addie. He kept making eye contact with me, and before I knew it, I was transformed into a señorita, too. Nancy got in the act, and it's a wonder we didn't knock anything off the food table. At the height of all the Volares, my aunt danced over to Stan and planted herself in front of him. She grabbed his shoulders and staged a hotsy-totsy little dance with him as though the rest of us were not even around.

Darlene cut in and we all laughed some more. At the final "Your love has given me wings" my aunt flapped her arms and took off across the lawn leaving us alone to giggle and finish up the song, each one of us having fun mimicking my aunt's dance moves.

I felt a little awkward when the music stopped. Nancy, Darlene, and I couldn't think of anything to say; we just giggled. Stan turned to me and said, "I see where you get your wild side." *My wild side? Stan thinks I have a wild side? Well, I guess I do, then.*

Darlene strolled over to Stan and announced, "I have a wild side, too." No one said anything, and I decided I needed to say something to fill the awkward silence.

"I guess we all have a wild side, dancing around like that. Especially Aunt Addie." Everyone burst out laughing again.

At the sound of her name, my aunt returned. "Are you girls making fun of me? I don't know whether that song is Spanish or Italian, but it makes the tiger in me come out. Grrr." Aunt Addie poured herself a glass of wine, and grabbed Stan's hand. "Come on soldier boy, let's you and Addie get acquainted over some of this good food." Stan shot an apologetic look at the rest of us as she led him away.

Nancy, Darlene, and I loaded up our plates and went off to sit by ourselves where we could make girl talk and relive the Volare dance. Every once in a while, I looked over to where my aunt had cornered Stan and found myself feeling a little jealous of her. I wondered how long it would be before he'd come my way again.

The party went along smoothly. My mother was in her glory buzzing from guest to guest. She looked particularly pretty in her rose-colored blouse and white pants. I think my father thought so too because he walked by her a couple of times stealing a kiss and patting her bottom. Darlene and Nancy and I practiced our dance moves and before long most of the guests were gyrating around the backyard. Danny Murphy arrived, and Nancy and Darlene started buzzing around him.

All the energy was exciting. Even my father didn't seem too upset that his pride and joy of a lawn was being demolished by eager dancers. My aunt danced up a storm with my brothers, while good-natured Stan was tossed between his aunt and Mrs. Kennedy. Every once in a while, he'd dance by me and twirl me around. The torches were lit, and the evening was charged with romance. I nudged the elastic fabric over my shoulders once again, but all my father had to do was come by and stare at me and I snapped it back into place.

All too soon, the crowd started to thin. Kisses and hugs were exchanged, and whispers of "this was the best party ever" floated between grateful guests. Neighbors shuffled back to their houses. Stan was one of the last to leave, and he asked me to walk him down the driveway.

"I had a really cool time," he said.

"Yeah, me too."

"Your aunt is a character."

"I told you she's the wild one in the family." I laughed.

"I don't know. I think you may have a little wild side yourself."

I felt my cheeks flush.

"Thanks for a good time, flirt." He bent over and kissed my forehead, and then he placed the back of his warm hand on my cheek before walking away. I watched him as he strolled toward Nancy's house. Midway there, he turned back. "Hey, don't get goofy on me. It's dark. Get in the house."

As I turned around to run to the front door, I noticed the outline of a figure standing in my bedroom window. It disappeared quickly behind the curtain, but I knew it was my aunt.

CHAPTER 6

The next day I couldn't wait to rehash the party with Darlene, but by the time all my chores were done and I had delivered clean plates back to neighbors, it was already after lunch. I held Mrs. Kennedy's cake platter until the end, so I could visit with Darlene for a while. But no one answered the Kennedys' door. Disappointed, I left the platter on the front porch so they would see it when they got home.

I thought I'd burst if I couldn't talk to someone, so I headed over to Nancy's. When I knocked on her door, the house was quiet except for the smooth sound of jazz rising from the backyard. I followed the sound and when I turned the corner, there stood a bare-chested Stan gripping the handle of a golf putter, intently concentrating on sinking a dimpled ball into a hole in the ground. Sweat glistened across his shoulders, muscles taut, he scooted the ball across the lush greenery of the Polankys' backyard. Tall boxwoods formed a perfect privacy hedge. Unlike the wide-open yards around it, theirs kept out neighborhood surveillance. When Stan sank the putt, I clapped. He jumped. "Oh, it's you! How long have you been there?"

"Long enough to know that ball didn't have a chance. Looks like fun. Where's everyone else?"

"Nancy and my aunt went shoe shopping. Uncle Vic is at work."

"Oh, okay. Well, will you tell Nancy I came by?"

"Sure, but you don't have to leave so soon."

"Oh. Well, I guess I could stay a little while." I grabbed a piece of hair from over my ear and started to play with it. It was a practiced gesture I had picked up from Darlene. Actually, she always looked cute when she did it. With me it was questionable.

Stan moved towards me. "Did I tell you what a neat party that was last night?"

"Yeah, I think you mentioned it," I chuckled.

"You looked real nice, too."

"Thanks." My stomach started to flutter.

"Can I get you a Coke?"

"Sure!"

Stan put down his club and ran into the house to get me a soda. I picked up the putter. The grip was still warm and a little moist, so I dried it with my shirt. I walked over to the ball and tapped it. It rolled towards the hole and stopped just short. I gave it another tap and it dropped in.

"Not bad. A real Sam Snead."

I looked up and smiled as Stan handed me the cold drink.

"Cheers." He clicked his bottle to mine.

I took a long sip and felt the fizz go up my nose. I let out a high-pitched hiccup. "Sorry. This always happens to me when I drink soda too fast." I covered my mouth as another hiccup escaped. "I can't stand it. It's so embarrassing."

"Don't apologize. I think it's cute," he said.

"You do?"

"Yeah, I do. As a matter of fact, I think everything about you is cute—real cute."

"Really?" My stomach tightened. This was getting interesting. I flicked my hair back over my ear and put my hand on my hip. I had once seen Doris Day do it, and it made her look fun and sassy. I looked him square in the eyes and smiled, but not so much that he would notice the chip in my front tooth.

"Adorable," he said. "And when you smile, you have the tiniest dimple in your cheek. It's like a little jewel." He touched my face. "I've always had a soft spot for girls with dimples."

Is this really happening to me? This gorgeous guy thinks my dimple is adorable and he likes my hiccups? Who likes hiccups? Okay, stay cool as if people say this stuff to you all the time. Just keep the conversation going.

"So how long have you been (hiccup) playing golf?"

"Since I was 15. My uncle taught me all I know. Want a lesson?" He picked up the club and handed it to me. "Let's work on your stance."

"My stance?"

"Yeah. How you should stand. Stand with your feet at shoulder's width and hold the club out in front of you."

Stan came up behind me and put his arms around me placing his hands over mine.

"Grip the club like this." I could smell his sweet sweat and the Coke on his breath. I started to feel hot all over and my hands began to quiver. I realized my hiccups had stopped but my heart raced. Stan's warm breath tickled my ear.

"Take your time. Relax and keep your eye on the ball. Then follow through. You seem tense."

"Who? Me?" I croaked.

"Just relax your neck and shoulders. Loosen up." He released the elastic in my ponytail. "That's better. Let your hair run free.

Ponytails are fine, but they pull on your neck." He massaged my neck. "You want your neck to be nice and loose."

He laid his face against mine. His fine whiskers pricked my cheek and my heart did a two-step in my chest. Part of me wanted to stay like this forever, and part of me wanted to run away. I had never been this close to a man before other than my father. My ears started to buzz a little. Stan got real quiet and then started to wiggle ever so slightly against my back. What was happening? I had to say something.

"Hey, it's hard enough for me to keep steady. Stop wiggling." I giggled.

He didn't say anything, just held onto me and the club real stiff-like. "Come on, flirt. Show me your form," he whispered in my ear.

Stan wiggled again, this time rubbing his body close—too close. I felt him hard against my spine. Something was different. I needed air. My ears grew hot and I needed to escape. What do I do? I had to do something, so I drew the club back and whacked the ball with all my might. Stan released me as the ball went flying into the hedges. He stepped back in surprise. I watched him as his eyes flickered and narrowed. He stared at me speaking only with hard eyes. I don't know why, but I started to laugh. Another look of surprise from him and I laughed even harder.

"What's wrong with you? It's not funny. Stop laughing! You're nothing more than a little tease."

I couldn't control myself. I laughed with the wild abandon of a toddler being tickled by a crazy uncle. I covered my mouth to make it stop, and I laughed through embarrassment and fear. I couldn't explain what just happened or what I was feeling, so I laughed. When Stan growled at me that I was just a little girl who needed to go home and grow up and then stormed into the house leaving me alone, I laughed some more.

And then I cried.

I realized all my cuteness was gone and I was too young and ugly and foolish for Stan. The only thing to do was to go home, because Stan wasn't coming back outside to flirt with me again. The golf pro had left the clubhouse.

This lesson was over.

CHAPTER 7

I stayed close to home for the next couple of days. Darlene and Nancy called a couple of times, but I pretended I had things to do. I didn't want to talk to anyone. I felt numb. Mom and Aunt Addie both asked me if something was wrong. Mom even checked my temperature in case I was coming down with something. She said my eyes looked funny. They did feel sore from the secret crying I had been doing, and my head ached a lot.

Aunt Addie tried her best to tell me funny cat stories to get me to laugh, but I was in no mood. I didn't want to tell Mom or my aunt what was really bothering me, because I knew Mom wouldn't be happy if she found out I was over at the Polanskys' house alone with Stan. And Aunt Addie might actually be happy that Stan thought I was too young for him. With me out of the way she could put the moves on him.

Thursday came and I couldn't stand the numbness anymore. I strapped on my roller skates. It felt good to feel the pavement rumbling beneath my feet. Harmonica Hill, the highest point around, one that had always threatened me as too steep, beckoned me. I scraped a path sideways to the top of the hill and pushed off. With knees bent and hands gripping my thighs, I whizzed down the hill with no idea as to how I would stop. The wind whipped my face and plastered my hair back. Midway down, I spotted a car making its way up the hill, and I was headed straight for it. No way to stop now. I veered to the right and tripped over a tar bubble. I went flying, my arms and legs flailing, and I landed on my knees.

The hot sting of flesh meeting pavement ripped through me. Tears streamed down my cheeks and blood dripped from my knees and elbows. Awful as it was, there was something strangely satisfying about the pain. It was the first time I had felt anything in the last three days. I hurt. I really hurt. But it wasn't the same. It was a physical hurt that gave me a reason to cry. I crouched on the side of the road and released a flood of tears, gulping in air. My body loosened and my headache lifted. Through the blur of tears, I stared up the long steep hill I had just descended. I tightened my skates, stood up and side-stepped my way back up.

For the rest of the afternoon I tore down Harmonica Hill. With each descent, I came down faster with more determination than the time before it. On my third try, I stopped falling. It's a good thing, because there wasn't much skin left on either of my knees. My arms and hands were battered and bruised. I knew I'd have scabs on me for weeks, but I didn't care. I could finally feel something again.

When I got home, I sneaked upstairs into the bathroom and applied antiseptic and Band-Aids to my arms and legs, and then I put on long-sleeved pajamas.

The next day I had a dentist appointment. Even though it was warm, I put on long pants and sleeves to hide my cuts. Just before I left to walk the seven blocks to Dr. Lerner's office,

Nancy called again. I told her I had a dentist appointment, and she told me she hoped he would get to the root of the problem.

"Very funny," I said as she snorted into the phone. Oh well, at least this time I didn't have to make up an excuse not to see her.

I strode down Hope Street past Bongo's. It was only 2:30 pm, and my appointment wasn't until 3:10, but I left a little early so that I could read the Archie comics Dr. Lerner always had in his waiting room. He had been my dentist for as long as I could remember, and I liked him until he started to drill. His hand shook terribly from some nervous condition, and more than once he had slipped and drilled my tongue. Every time I complained to my mother she said, "It's a small price to pay for a dentist who lets us make payments each month for our rotten teeth."

I didn't see the red sedan until it was right alongside me. It coasted up slowly and stopped. There sat Stan with his sunglasses and a smile. My stomach did a flip. "Hi flirt. Going my way?" I couldn't believe he was smiling and talking to me. "Nancy mentioned you were on your way to the dentist. I thought I could give a cute girl like you a lift, if you're still talking to me that is. Not that I'd blame you if you never spoke to me again after what I said. I was a jerk." He peeked over his sunglasses with gorgeous puppy-dog eyes.

Stan was apologizing to me? He wanted to make things right between us? "You weren't a jerk. I shouldn't have interrupted the lesson that way. I just never had a golf lesson before, and I wasn't sure what you wanted me to do."

"Well, I'd really like to make it up to you by giving you a ride the rest of the way."

"Uh, that's okay, I can walk. My parents don't let me drive with anyone but them." As soon as I spoke the words, I realized how dumb that sounded. Just like a little girl.

Stan smiled. "Well, they know me. And I am a super-responsible driver. It's not like I'm a stranger or anything. Actually, after Sunday night I'm what you'd call a family friend." He waited. "I'd really like to talk to you a little about the other day… and I think you owe it to me. I won't tell your parents, if that's what you're worried about. It would give us a few minutes to talk, boyfriend to girlfriend." He jumped out of the car and I watched as he bowed and opened the passenger door for me.

This is right out of the movies. He wants to talk boyfriend to girlfriend. I think I do owe it to him. Look at him. He's so handsome. I guess I am important to him. He placed a gentle hand on my shoulder, removed his sunglasses, and gave me a long, pleading look. I looked around to see if anyone I knew was watching. The coast was clear. I slipped into the front seat. Stan gave a quick look up and down the street, put his sunglasses back on, and hopped back into the driver's side. We glided down Hope Street. I showed him where Dr. Lerner's office was, and he pulled to the curb.

"What time's your appointment?" he asked.

"Ten after 3."

"We still have twenty minutes. We could go for a little spin and talk."

"Sure!" I said. I was relaxed now, and feeling so much better—even lighter. Stan was himself again. I knew he wouldn't let me be late for my appointment. This sure beat reading comic books.

We continued up Hope Street past storefronts and headed out past Woodway Golf Course. Stan turned the radio to a station I didn't recognize. The music sounded like what he was listening to in his backyard when he tried to teach me how to golf. "What kind of music is this?" I asked.

"Jazz. Ya like it?"

"Yeah, it's kind of nice." I cranked open the passenger window. Warm air caressed my hair and neck.

Soon Stan turned into the ballpark where my brothers always played their Little League games. No one was around. "This looks like a nice place to talk," he said. He pulled up under a tree and turned off the engine. I watched as he removed his sunglasses, ran his fingers over his crewcut, and rested his head on the back of the seat. "Why don't you move over a little closer," he said. "You seem so far away. But before you do, close the window, would you? It's getting a little chilly." He rolled up the driver's window.

"Sure." I immediately cranked up my side window and inched over a little. "So, you wanted to talk?"

"Yeah. I want to apologize for those things I said to you the other day. I feel real bad about it. Do you forgive me?"

"Of course, I do." I smiled.

"See? Right there. When you smile, you are so cute. And you are so understanding. I've never met anyone like you before." He reached for my hand. "The artist in me wants to sketch that smile of yours. From here to here." He brushed his finger across my mouth, his eyes lingering on my lips. A surge of heat coursed through me.

"Sure," I said.

"And maybe you'll wear that pretty little white blouse you wore the other night and show me those soft shoulders of yours?" Stan's eyes bore into me as he moved his warm finger down the side of my neck and across my right shoulder. His eyes flickered for a moment.

I started to feel a little embarrassed or something—sort of like the other day in Nancy's backyard when I wanted to run away. I willed myself to stay cool. "Maybe we ought to get going. I don't want to be late for my appointment."

"Don't worry. I'm sure your dentist has kept you waiting before and didn't give it a second thought. After all, I thought our talk was important to you." He inched closer and put his hand on my thigh.

I stared at it. His hand burned through my pants leg. *What am I doing? My parents will kill me if they find out.*

"I really should be getting over to the dentist office." I tried to act nonchalant.

"Like I said, the dentist can wait. We just got here." He reached for my hand again. I swallowed. My pulse throbbed in my throat, and my ears rang.

"You know, you look tired. Why don't you stay and take a nap? I can walk. It's not too far." I slid over and reached for the door handle.

Through the window I saw a man walking his dog toward us. Stan grabbed my arm and pulled me toward him. "Not so fast. I'm not finished talking to you yet." His face changed into the scary, angry look he had the other day in the Polanskys' backyard. His hand captured mine in a steely grip.

Oh no! What do I do? He's hurting me. Stan's hurting me!

Stan's eyes cut past me as he spotted the man walking his dog through the park. I reached across Stan and pushed the horn, and then turned to the man and his dog and waved. The man responded with a smile and a quick wave as he hustled past us.

Stan straightened and released me. "Do you know him?"

"Yeah, that's Linda Carson's dad. Hi, Mr. Carson," I yelled to the strange man and his dog through the closed window, all the while waving at him as if I were the village idiot.

Stan threw his sunglasses back on and checked his watch. He gave me one of his sweet Stan smiles. "You know, you're right. It is getting close to your appointment. I better get you over there, or you'll never want to have anything to do with me again." He winked at me, then gave me a quick kiss on the forehead, and turned on the ignition.

As we drove toward Dr. Lerner's office, Stan became chatty, and I started to relax again.

"There's a place I found in the woods the other day when I went sketching. It's behind the Kennedy's house. Just past that old tire swing there's a small path that leads to a clearing. Do you know it?"

I brightened. "Yeah, Darlene and I picnic there a lot."

"Then I'll meet you there Monday at 10 am. I'm serious about sketching that beautiful smile. Okay?"

"Uh, sure."

As I jumped out of the car in front of the dentist's office, Stan delivered one of his melt-my-heart grins. "Hey, flirt. Take care of that smile for me."

I ran up the steps to the dentist's office rubbing my sore arm and looked at the clock. 3:10 pm exactly.

That afternoon when Dr. Lerner drilled away, it hardly hurt at all. My mind was on other things.

CHAPTER 8

Saturday morning brought with it a family field trip to Stanton State Park that had the largest swimming pool I had ever seen. Dad packed us into our family station wagon. Mom and Aunt Addie sat up front with him, and I claimed a window seat in the back so that I could keep my eyes looking out the front to avoid getting car sick. Corey and Michael amused themselves by trading baseball cards and chomping on wads of Bazooka. Although my eyes were staring out the window at the scenery, my mind was miles away daydreaming about Stan and our secret date.

"You're awfully quiet back there, Bibi," ventured Dad.

I met his eyes in the rearview mirror and gave him a smile. "Just listening to everyone else talking. That's all. Don't want to miss a word."

"A certain young man wouldn't have anything to do with it, would he?" Mom teased.

I felt my face redden.

"I saw Danny Murphy giving you the eyes the other night at the party."

"Danny Murphy?? Ewww! Cooties." I moaned.

"Bibi and Danny sittin' in the tree. K-I-S-S-I-N-G," Michael sang.

"Mom, tell him to stop!"

"First comes love. Then comes marriage. Then comes Bibi with the baby carriage!" Corey added in his best sing-songy voice before crowing with laughter.

"All right boys, that's enough," Dad warned.

I looked over at my little brothers who had curled up their lips like monkeys. I held up my fist as I mouthed to both of them. "You're gonna get it."

"Mom! Bibi's threatening us."

"No threat. It's a promise, you two nitwits."

"Okay, you three. Calm down. We're almost there," my father admonished.

The park came into view with its rolling green golf course, nature trails, picnic areas, and our favorite pool. I looked forward to this trip every year. Everyone settled into such a good mood. It was a day of sheer relaxation when my father was not allowed to speak about his work at the print shop. This year would be even sweeter with Aunt Addie along.

We spread our blanket out and set up some lawn chairs under a large elm. We had established our base. This was the spot where we would picnic after we had enough of the pool. The trees gave off ample shade to cover Dad. No matter how much my mother nagged him to cover up, he always went home with a sunburned face and back.

I couldn't wait to get to the pool. This would be my first swim of the season. "Let's hurry up, everybody. We need to get our pool passes before it gets crowded," I called.

We all hustled over to the pool and each paid a quarter for the green ankle bracelet that gave us each a locker for our clothes and carte blanche to swim all day. I ran to the locker room and changed into my bathing suit. My legs and elbows were still covered with large, reddish-brown scabs. Not the most attractive sight, but nothing was going to keep me from that pool.

By the time I emerged from the locker room, the boys were already changed and waiting to go in. Mom and Dad and Aunt Addie had found a free table with an umbrella and laid out towels and a bowl of pretzels to snack on until lunch.

Dad let out a low whistle when I passed by him with my scabby body parts. "Whoa! What does the other guy look like?"

I felt my face redden. "I took a couple of tumbles on my skates yesterday. They still sort of sting."

"Too many twirls and crossovers?" my aunt teased.

I rolled my eyes. "Maybe."

"Remember to get out of the pool when your teeth start to chatter," my mother warned. "The sun will warm you up. And don't go in the deep end. I just got my hair done, and I don't want to get it wet going in after you kids. Bibi, keep an eye on your brothers. You're the big sister. And don't let them—"

"Mary, relax. The kids will be fine," my aunt said. "Bibi will keep an eye on them, and we're right here."

My mother cocked an eyebrow at my aunt. "Easy enough for you to say. You, who never learned to swim."

I smiled at my aunt who just shrugged her shoulders, removed her cover-up, and draped herself across one of the chairs. She looked like a movie star in her green flowered two-piece, sunglasses, and wide-brimmed straw hat. Aunt Addie didn't have to swim. It was enough that she sat poolside and jazzed the place up. She was all glamour.

My father had lost no time in making himself comfortable. He was already stretched out on a chaise lounge with his eyes closed under his sunglasses, a denim golf cap perched on his head to cover the small bald spot he refused to admit to.

Mom waved us all away and settled into the chair next to Aunt Addie. My mother's navy-blue suit with a wide band of white across the middle accentuated her tiny waist. She stretched out her long, freckled legs that Dad always bragged about. He teased her that they were "the snappiest set of legs in the neighborhood—perfect for hitchhiking." She always pretended to be insulted, but I think she secretly liked to hear it.

I held my nose and jumped into the pool. Michael and Corey cannonballed after me. I surveyed the pool searching for older kids. Most of them were in the deep end beyond the string of blue floating balls, but I spotted a few others nearby and decided to swim closer to them in hopes of getting away from my little brothers and their dumb game of seeing who could spit water the farthest through the gaps in their front teeth.

As soon as I got close to a girl I judged to be about my age, she stopped what she was doing and smiled a hello. I smiled back.

"Brrr. This water's cold," I said.

"It's not so bad once you get used to it." She grinned through a pair of braces. She introduced herself as Janet and I told her my name.

"The reason I'm in this end of the pool is because I'm watching those two apes over there." I pointed to my brothers and rolled my eyes.

She smiled and pointed to her little brother. "That's my ape over there." She mimicked my eye rolling and sighed.

At that, a stream of water spouted from my brothers' direction and hit me square across the bridge of my nose. I glared at Corey who emitted one of his hyena laughs. "Stop it, you creep." More hyena yips. Corey edged closer sending more water projectiles my way.

"Ew!" Janet squealed and stepped back.

Sizing up the situation, I decided I needed to put a quick halt to it or I would lose Janet's interest altogether. I grabbed Corey's head and forced it underwater. I held it until he was grabbing at my hand. When he came up he was gasping for breath. "I'm telling," he whined and quickly dogpaddled away to report the incident to my mother.

"He won't be bothering us anymore." I looked at Janet and we both laughed.

"Brothers!" We both spoke at the same time. "Thumbs, thumbs, I hope it comes." We grabbed each other's hands and pressed our thumbs together.

"Ha! You remind me of my friend, Darlene. We do that all the time."

"Yeah, I do it with my friend, Carla, too." Janet said.

That was when I heard it. My mother's high-pitched cry. "Uh! Uh!" I turned to the sound just in time to see her sailing through the air and plunging into the deep end of the pool. New hairdo and all, she headed towards a slice of bright blue and white striped fabric that could only be Michael's bathing suit. I froze. My heart raced as my eyes frantically searched the pool for Corey. I spotted him clinging to the side, tracking my mother. Everything seemed to be happening in slow motion.

My aunt yelled hysterically to the lifeguard pointing and screaming. "Help! Over there! A little boy is drowning!" Then she shook my father who had already fallen into a restful snooze. "Billy! Billy! Help Mary!"

Just as my father shot out of his lounge chair ready for action, my mother surfaced with Michael who hit the air coughing, sputtering, and crying, all the while clinging to her neck. The lifeguard swam over and calmly peeled Michael off my mother and floated him to the side of the pool. Mom followed behind and pulled herself out.

As she started to stand, her right leg slipped and folded under her. She toppled over and crashed hard on her leg and rolled onto her backside. Oomph! My mother, a hero only seconds before, collapsed in pain on the cement pool deck in front of everybody. Dad and Aunt Addie rushed over, while I climbed out of the pool abandoning Janet.

"Oh, Billy, it hurts," my mother whimpered. "I think I broke it." She held her leg and started to cry.

"Can you move it?" my father asked.

"Barely. It hurts. Oh Billy, what have I done?"

Dad held Mom's head, caressing her wet hair and face. "Try to take some deep breaths, sweetheart."

The rest of it was a blur. Someone called an ambulance. A policeman came, too. Dad handed the car keys to my aunt and then hopped into the ambulance with Mom. The policeman offered to stay behind while we gathered our belongings and led my aunt to the hospital. Corey and Michael drove with the policeman. Ten minutes later, I stood with my brothers and aunt in the waiting room of the emergency room of Saint Francis Hospital in Poughkeepsie, New York.

After waiting for what seemed like an eternity for word on my mother, Dad came into the waiting room and announced that Mom had broken her leg and would be wearing a cast for a while.

"Cool!" Cory whispered.

I glared at him, but couldn't shake my feelings of guilt. If I had been watching both my brothers, Michael wouldn't have had a close call, and my mother wouldn't have broken her leg.

Dad disappeared again and returned after a while with Mom. She hobbled in on crutches, sporting a long white cast on her right leg. She gave a pathetic smile that I couldn't bear to look at. A lump rose in my throat, and I found myself fighting back tears. Corey and Michael both rushed to her for a hug, but Dad intercepted. "Everyone needs to be careful and gentle around Mommy."

"Mommy, does it hurt?" I asked in my softest voice.

"Right now it seems like a huge numb club. But look at me with my crutches. No one will dare get out of line now." She waved one of the crutches at us.

We laughed, because that's what she wanted us to do. But I really didn't feel like laughing.

Dad took it real slow on the ride home. Mom sat in the back with the boys so she and her cast had a little more room to stretch out. Aunt Addie and I sat in the front.

It was a long ride home, but when Mom was comfortably seated in the living room with her leg propped up, and the boys ran outside to blab about the day to everyone in the neighborhood, my mother asked the inevitable question. "Billy, what will we do? Next Monday is your traffic court date, and if you lose your license, I can't drive."

"What? You think you still can't hitchhike with one leg?" he teased.

"I'm not kidding. What will we do?" my mother moaned.

"Easy. I'll bring you along to court and plead with the judge. Then my father got down on both knees and folded his hands in mock prayer. "Your Honor, please. What can I do with a wife who has lost her best hitchhiking leg to a tragic pool accident? How will she taxi herself and our three kids around town?"

Aunt Addie roared at my father's insanity.

"Billy! I'm serious!" my mother said.

"Mary, you worry too much. We'll figure something out." He got up off his knees.

"Maybe I can help," Aunt Addie said.

"No, Addie, you have a business to run in California. I'm not going to ask you to spend your summer as our chauffeur," my mother said.

"You don't have to ask. I'm offering. You're going to need some extra help around the house for a while, peg leg. And that's what sisters are for."

"I can't—"

"I don't want to hear anything more about it. Jane is running the shop alone now and hasn't once sent up a distress signal. She loves doing it and will appreciate the opportunity. As for me, I'll have extra time with my sister and her family."

My father and mother looked at each other a long time. Dad spoke first. "Thank you, Adeline. We would truly appreciate it." And then he quipped, "I don't care what everyone else says about you, you're okay in my book."

"Oh, you...," she raised her fist at him and we all laughed.

And that's how it happened that my only aunt ended up spending the entire summer with us. And that's when the *real* craziness began.

CHAPTER 9

Mom stayed home from church with Aunt Addie the next day, while my father took the rest of us off to 9 o'clock mass. I was still feeling pretty guilty about causing my mother's broken leg, so I asked Dad if I could light a candle for "a special intention." I think he knew why, but didn't let on.

We stopped by Elizabeth's Bakery on the way home and picked up the best sticky buns in town. When we got home the table was set, and the smells of bacon and coffee wafted their way through the house. My mother sat in the living room with a pillow elevating her broken leg. A glass of orange juice stood on a snack table in front of her.

My aunt came around the corner with a platter of pancakes. "Just in time. Did you say 'Hi' to God for me?" she chirped.

"Yes, and God said your name sounded familiar, but he couldn't quite place the face," Dad said.

Aunt Addie shot back. "Well for heaven's sake, you should go back and invite him for breakfast. I'm sure he remembers my blueberry pancakes. Maybe he could even work a miracle on my sister's bum leg while he's here."

"All right, you two. Quit your sniping," my mother said. "Someone bring me some pancakes and bacon before they get cold."

I prepared a plate for my mother, added a sticky bun, and walked it over to her. "I lit a candle for you at church today, Mom."

"Thanks, sweetie. I'm feeling better already."

After breakfast and the dishes were done, we all settled into our usual routines. Dad and Mom read the paper. Aunt Addie poured herself another cup of tea and went out on the back porch to sit in the sun and read. The boys met up with their friends for a game of baseball in the street, and I slipped off to my bedroom to lay out my outfit for the next day's art session with Stan.

Since he had requested I wear the blouse I wore the night of the party, I decided on the identical outfit. The only thing missing was Darlene's locket. I zipped across the street to borrow it.

When I got there, Mrs. Kennedy wanted to know all about the accident and how my mother was doing. Somehow Mrs. Kennedy also knew about my father's speeding ticket. She never missed a trick. "Tell your mother I'd offer to help with driving duties if I didn't have so many pressing volunteer commitments, dear."

"Thanks, Mrs. Kennedy, but my aunt's staying on to help us."

"Darlene is still upstairs. That girl needs a firecracker put under her to get her to move some mornings."

I found Darlene still stretched out on her bed, surrounded by her adoring stuffed animals. She was just finishing up an entry in her diary, which she quickly shoved into the top drawer under her underwear when she saw me.

"Bibi, that is so awful about your mother. What happened?" I repeated the story I had just finished telling her mother and finished up with how my aunt had offered to stay for as long as she was needed.

"Before I forget it, may I borrow your locket? I'm wearing my white blouse tomorrow, and it goes great with it," I said.

"Sure." Darlene said. "You know this means I get to borrow your charm bracelet whenever I want." She held the locket in her hand until I agreed.

"Deal." I put my palm out and she placed the locket in it. "So, what are you doing today?" I asked.

"The same old thing—dinner at my grandmother's house. Visiting with my cousins."

"Is your little cousin Jeannie going to be there?"

"Of course. And she'll be following me around listening to all my conversations, begging to let her brush my hair and to try on my shoes."

I giggled. "I wish I had cousins. My only relative sort of close to my age is my Aunt Addie. I'd like to talk about boys, but she isn't even dating anyone."

"I think she has her eye on Stan. Did you see them at your party? They would make such a cute couple."

I froze. "Stan? And my aunt? I think he was just being polite."

"That's not how people are *polite* to each other. That's how people *flirt* with each other, dodo bird. Just think. Stan could be your future uncle. He would make such a dreamy uncle." She gazed off and fake-fanned her face as if she were some southern belle calling for vapors.

No! She has it all wrong! Stan was flirting with me! I saw how my aunt tried to steal him away at the party, but he always came back to me. Darlene doesn't know anything.

"I have to go now. I told my mother I wouldn't be too long," I lied. "Thanks for the locket."

"See you Tuesday night at the church skating party!" She yelled after me as I hurried out of her room.

"Yeah, sure." I darted across the street and bounded up to my room, clutching the locket. I placed it on the corner of the vanity that was always cluttered these days with Aunt Addie's stash of perfume and creams and lipsticks. Her bed was still unmade and a wet beach towel sat in a clump on the floor next to a waste basket brimming with lipstick-stained tissues, old notes to herself, receipts and packaging from little souvenirs she had purchased at Bongo's. And there lay another empty bottle of mouthwash with flakes of orange and rosebud potpourri tossed on top of it.

Yuck! Why can't she clean up after herself? What am I, her slave? This is my room and I'm sharing it with her. Aren't grownups supposed to be neater than kids? This was fun at first, but now my room looks like Filene's Basement on a Christmas sale day. And I can't stand the smell of all that potpourri.

I emptied the wastebasket and locked my bedroom door. I walked over to the vanity and picked up my aunt's rouge and dabbed a little on my cheeks. I ran the pink frosted lipstick across my mouth. "War paint. This is war! And I'm defending my man," I said to my reflection in the mirror. I picked up her orange rat-tailed comb and teased the top of my hair the way I had seen her do it. Not bad. I changed into my white blouse, secured Darlene's locket around my neck, and as the finishing touch pulled the blouse down to expose my bare shoulders. I practiced how I would pose for Stan the next day.

The door handle moved and then stopped. Another try and then my aunt's voice. "Bibi? May I come in?"

"Uh…sure. Just a minute. I grabbed a tissue and swiped my cheeks and lips. I patted my hair down, raised the shoulders on my blouse and scurried to the door, trying my best to act normal. I opened the door, feeling a little awkward. "Sorry. Sometimes I just like to keep those two pesky brothers out." I kept my eyes down so my aunt couldn't see I was lying. If I have learned nothing else about my aunt and my mother, it is how quick they are to figure things out. My aunt gave me a once over and smirked.

"Yeah, I can only imagine how pesky those boys can be to a grown-up big sister, but if you need a little privacy from your old aunt, I get it. And by the way, if you ever want to dabble with my makeup, feel free."

I felt my face flush. "Thanks."

"I'd be happy to teach you some of my techniques, just as long as you don't let on to your mother. She'd have my head."

"Yeah, she likes to think of me as her little girl. I *am* getting old enough to wear some lipstick and stuff."

"Sit down." Aunt Addie patted the chair to the vanity. She walked to the door and turned the lock. "Got to keep those pesky boys away." She grinned. Then she returned to open the top of her makeup bag. "Now, let's start with a little foundation."

By the time my aunt had taken me from foundation to eyeliner application, to the appropriate height to tease hair my length, I no longer looked twelve. Staring back at me in the mirror was someone who looked at least seventeen. I liked the result…sort of. My mother definitely could not see me like this.

My aunt seemed pleased with the transformation and left me alone to bask in the new me. She took her makeup bag and headed for the bathroom to freshen up. I strutted around the room practicing my posing. I changed my outfit to preserve it for the next day, but decided to keep the makeup on for a while.

Getting by my mother and escaping out the side kitchen door was a trick I had mastered. I skipped back over to Darlene's, but she had already left for her grandmother's. No cars at Nancy's either. I went into the garage and slipped on my skates, tightened them and placed my twine necklace with the skate key on it around my neck. I skated a couple of blocks over to Woodside Street where I knew I wouldn't be bothered or noticed.

Woodside Street was one of my favorite places to skate. It had no cracks in the sidewalks. New concrete provided smooth skating and the perfect area to practice quick turns and skating backwards. All I could think about was my date with Stan the next day.

As if thinking so much about him made him magically appear, I looked up and there came his car cruising down Woodside Street towards me, windows open, the sound of jazz spilling out onto the street. My heart raced and my stomach did cartwheels as I waited for him to slow down. The car wasn't slowing. I smiled and waved and he looked right at me and kept on driving. I waved harder and called out his name. The brake lights came on and he slowly backed up. I skated over to his opened window. His eyes combed over me. He had a strange, startled look on his face.

"Hi. How are you? I didn't know it was you. You look different...older," he said.

"Really? Oh, I just decided to put a little makeup on. My aunt is teaching me." I raised my hand to my hair.

"It figures. Your aunt...." He stopped.

"My aunt what?"

"Nothing. It's just that, well, not every girl needs makeup. You're a natural beauty. Nothing needs to go on that beautiful canvas of yours. He ran his hand across my cheek.

"I think it makes me look pretty grown up." I touched my face. "You don't like it?"

"Hey, come here." He stretched his hand out to me. "I didn't mean to hurt your feelings."

"Oh, you didn't." I reached into my pocket and found an old balled up piece of tissue and started scrubbing my face with it. "We were only playing around with it. 'Ya know. Every once in a while, we like to get silly and pretend we're clowns. I didn't realize I still had it on."

Stan's shoulders relaxed, and he smiled one of his mysterious smiles. "Yeah, I can imagine you as a cute little clown. You're such a little show-off." He pressed his finger to the tip of my nose.

I looked down at the tissue, which was now smeared with streaks of red, green, and black. "There. Is it gone?" I asked.

"Almost. Come here." He reached into his pocket and pulled out the softest cotton handkerchief I have ever felt and wet it with his peppermint spit. He held my chin in one warm hand. I closed my eyes, and in front of all of Woodside Street, my heart racing and my thighs electrically charged, I let "my Stan" gently rub the color off my face.

"There. All done," he said as he finished the final swipe. "Can I give you a lift home?"

I wanted to rip off my skates and hop into the car alongside him, but knew I would be in trouble if I accepted a ride to my house with him.

"Thanks anyway, but I need to practice my twirls. Wednesday night is the skating party in our church parking lot, and I'm a little rusty."

"Oh yeah. Nancy was talking about that. I think she's going, too."

"Oh, she'll be there. You should come, too. It's a lot of fun." I said.

"Maybe I will. I don't skate, but it might be fun to watch."

"I could teach you."

"I'm sure you could. I bet you could teach me a lot, but I'm better at watching." He gave me the up and down again, and I felt little electrical charges go through me. "Are we still on for our art session tomorrow?" he added.

"Sure. Can't wait."

He reached for my twine necklace that held my skate key and pulled me toward him. "Neither can I. You're the perfect model…the face of an angel and the body of a dancer."

Again, he raked his eyes over my body. I got a little nervous, so I skated back to the safety of the sidewalk. I turned back to him, and as casually as I could, I yelled, "Okay, see you tomorrow at 10." I charged down the sidewalk and glided into the most fantastic twirl I had ever executed. I looked back to see if he caught it, but he had already turned the corner. I would just need to wait until Wednesday night's skating party. Then Stan could watch all he wanted.

CHAPTER 10

When I woke up the next morning Mom, Dad, and Aunt Addie were having breakfast. I hopped downstairs, anxious for ten o'clock to come so I could sneak off and meet Stan for my sketching date. My father and aunt were already dressed while Mom sat in her robe with her leg elevated.

"Oh, good. You're awake," my mother said as I sat down at the table. "Your aunt and father are almost ready to leave. I'm glad your father got a friend of his to help push his court date up so he can get this over with. Addie is going with him, and I'm going to need my Bibi to wait on me and help with the boys while they're gone."

"Wait! I have plans." I looked at my father. "How long will you be gone?"

"This could take some time. My friend said Monday mornings are usually busy, so I don't know how many cases are on the docket."

"Well, I mean…do you think you'll be back by 10?"

"I'm scheduled for 9. We may be. But I wouldn't bet the ranch on it, kiddo. Why?"

"I told you. I have plans…with Darlene."

My mother jumped in, "What plans?"

My mind raced for a plausible fib. "I promised her I'd help her create a scrapbook for her father for his birthday. We're meeting at her house at 10."

My mother looked at my father and then at me. "Well, this is the first I've heard about it. You'll just have to ask Darlene to bring the materials over here so that you can work here. I can help, too. I used to be pretty good at scrapbooking."

I started to pace. "Darlene has too many materials to bring over. I can't ask her to cart everything over here just because I need to babysit my mother," I argued. "It's not fair…to Darlene!"

My mother and aunt glared at me. My father's face reddened and his eyes narrowed. "I'll tell you what's not fair, young lady. What's not fair is that your poor mother is sitting at home with a cast up to her thigh because you were too irresponsible to keep an eye on your brothers at the pool! You're to stay in this house, not 'babysitting' your mother, but caring for her until your aunt and I return. And when I do return, you better have changed your attitude." Then my father turned to my aunt. "Adeline, if you're ready, we'll go."

My aunt picked up her purse, cocked her head in my direction, and gave me one more stern look as she followed my father out the door.

I felt sick and my stomach flopped. Everybody *did* blame me for my mother's accident. I had just told my parents an awful lie, and I was sure to miss my date with Stan. I walked to the window and watched as my father's car rolled out of sight.

My throat felt tight and lumpy. Tears blurred my eyes. What a mess I had made of everything. I sunk into the living room chair and brooded in silence while my mother didn't say a word—she didn't have to. I put my head into my hands and sobbed. I wanted to run to my mother and ask her forgiveness and tell her the truth, but I knew she would become even angrier. I had always told my mother everything, and I wanted so much to tell her about Stan.

After a few minutes of silence, I heard my mother release a soft sigh and shuffle to get up. I snapped to attention and wiped my eyes on my shirt. "Mommy, do you need something?"

"Another cup of tea would be nice." Maybe you'd like to join me? Things don't seem so bad after a warm cup of tea."

"Sure. I'll make it. How about some toast and jelly, too?" I asked.

"Yes, I think toast and jelly is just what the doctor ordered." She smiled.

We sat at the table for at least half an hour, healing our wounds. I couldn't say much for fear of telling another lie. My mother did most of the talking. She told me how annoyed she was over Dad's speeding ticket and how annoyed she was with herself for slipping at the pool.

She never said a word about how it was my fault; I just knew she was thinking it. She offered again to let me have Darlene come over to work on the scrapbook at our house. I couldn't look her in the eyes when I told her it was okay and that Darlene could do it herself.

"Oh," was all she said.

I cleaned up the breakfast dishes and yelled to my brothers to get dressed. Then I brought my mother a small basin of warm water and a washcloth with her toothbrush and comb so she could freshen up. She gave a sweet smile when I handed her a small mirror and her favorite Rose of Sharon lipstick.

While mom washed up, I slipped upstairs to shower and primp. It gave me a chance to steal a few more peeks out the window at Stan's car. I donned "my special Stan outfit" just in case Dad surprised me and came home early. I figured I might still be able to keep my appointment.

At 9 o'clock I thought of my father and wondered how his court hearing was going. At 9:45 I caught a glimpse of Stan loading what looked like a picnic basket into the trunk of his car, and then he pulled away. I wondered why he took his car when he could have just walked up to the woods.

My stomach jumped again with a case of the nerves, and I watched the clock as minute after minute ticked away. By 10 o'clock I was frantic. "Why isn't Daddy home?" I asked my mother. "Is there any chance he'll go to jail?"

"No. I'm sure your father and Addie will be here soon," Mom said. "Maybe they had to wait longer than they thought."

"But they had an appointment. Wouldn't the judge keep his appointment?"

"Well, that was probably just an approximate time. The judge needed to be sure your father would be there when he called his name. These things take time." Mom sounded so knowledgeable. I couldn't help but wonder how *she* knew about these things.

At 10:15 AM, I looked out the window to see if Stan's car had come back. Nope. That could only mean he was still waiting for me. I wondered how long he would wait before he'd give up.

Mom kept eyeing me. "Bibi, why don't you dust the living room and dining room? No use wasting all that pent-up energy."

By 11 o'clock, Dad and Aunt Addie still weren't home, and Stan's car was still missing. How long would this waiting go on? At 11:15, I heard my father's car turn onto the gravel drive-way. *Finally!*

I peeked out the front door to see Aunt Addie getting out of the driver's side. Car doors slammed, and Dad and my aunt both came through the front door. My father grumbled "Just as I thought—thirty days as a pedestrian." And then he headed to the refrigerator to pour himself some iced tea. Then he sat down at the dining room table winding up to deliver the play-by-play description of his day in court. Normally I would have been hanging on his every word, but I had places to go. I gave a quick goodbye and took off out the front door.

I zoomed away rehearsing how I would explain my late arrival to Stan. I made a beeline straight up the path through the woods to our meeting place. No Stan. I looked around and called his name. No response. He was gone. I sat down on a rock in defeat.

A square imprint of crushed grass caught my eye. *That must be where he laid out the picnic and waited for me. Poor Stan. I kept him waiting too long and he thought I wasn't coming. How will I make this up to him?* Three cigarette butts lay on the ground. *He waited through three smokes for me.* I picked one up to see if it was still warm. Cold.

I need to find him. He'll forgive me when he learns I was stuck at home with my mother. I'll even tell him about my father's court date if I have to. I need to find him and make this right.

I ran down the path in the opposite direction until I reached Harmonica Hill. *That's where he must have parked—the street behind the woods.* No car. I scurried down the street to see if he had parked further away. No Stan. He was gone for sure. I had to find him. I retraced my tracks and raced back through the woods, past our meeting spot, and back to my house and into the garage.

My old green Schwinn bicycle lay on its side, discarded and dusty from no use. It was way too small but it would have to do. Too much territory to cover on roller skates. I hopped on my bike and pedaled off, heading down McGillicutty across to Palmer Street. Scanning the area, I plowed across Woodside and trudged down Hope Street past the movie theater and the bowling alley, checking frantically for any sign of Stan's car. I skirted across store parking lots and past Springdale Diner and The Fudge Shop. No Stan. *Where could he be?* Passing Dr. Lerner's office, I headed for the ball field we had gone to just a few days ago for our private talk. The field was deserted. I rode over to the place under the tree where we had parked just days before and laid the bike down. I needed to catch my breath and think. Sweat dripped from my forehead, and my bangs curled. Beads of moisture covered my upper lip and chest. I had to find Stan.

Ten minutes later I had cooled down but couldn't think of anywhere else to go except back to McGillicutty to wait for him to come home. *What if he came home when I was out looking for him?* The thought drove me into a panic again. I hopped on my bike and took off again. This time I drove further down Hope Street and then I spotted him—his car at least. It was parked in front of Kirby's Bar and Grill. A fluorescent blinking martini glass flashed like a beacon from the bar's window. It would take all my courage to walk through the weathered wood door.

Propping my bike against a fire hydrant, I watched as a couple of customers went in and a lone customer came out. I walked over to the window and stood on tiptoes to peek in. I had never seen the inside of a bar before. I had never even been this close to one. Through the cloudy filmy windows I could barely make out anything. The sun beat at my back, sending a glare across the glass. I shaded the sides of my eyes with my hands like a pair of binoculars and pressed my forehead against the grimy windows.

By squinting I could make out the outline of five customers who sat with their backs to me nestled up to the bar. A woman who looked like my aunt slipped into the restroom. Standing behind the bar, facing his customers was Mr. Kirby himself; I recognized him from church. He spied me almost immediately and scowled. Pointing at me, I watched as he said something to the other men at the bar who turned in unison and stared out at me. One of them was Stan. He didn't get up. He just glared at me. I tapped on the window and motioned for him to come out. The other men looked at Stan who just shrugged his shoulders and turned away. I rapped on the window again. Mr. Kirby flung his white bartending towel across the bar and stormed out the front door.

"What do you think you're doin' here, girlie?"

"I need to talk to my friend."

"There's no one in there who wants anything to do with you, so scram!"

"But Stan…"

Mr. Kirby gave me a dark look and folded his arms across his chest. "Scram."

I got on my bicycle and pedaled away.

When I arrived home I decided to stand watch until Stan came home. Then I would explain. I patrolled the street pedaling back and forth, back and forth until my calves cramped so much I had to put my bicycle away. I stationed myself on my front step. My stomach growled, but I refused to leave my post to feed it.

Corey passed by a few times before sitting down next to me. "What are you doin'? Posin' for animal crackers?" he teased.

"Oh, you're so funny I forgot to laugh." I scrunched up my face and crossed my eyes.

My brother let out a snort when he saw my face. "Do that again."

I mustered up a dopier look this time and he laughed harder. I couldn't keep from giggling too. We sat there making faces at each other, and I felt my body start to relax.

Corey sniffed the air. "You really smell, 'ya know. You need a bath."

"Get lost, you creep." I took an imaginary swipe at him.

As soon as my brother left, I stole a sniff under my arms. The aroma *was* a little strong. *I better put some powder under my armpits, or when Stan comes home, he'll smell me, too.*

I came through the front door; I saw my aunt jiggling around in front of our television, watching a music and dance show. "Isn't American Bandstand the best show around?" she called to me across the room. My mother was seated in a chair with her leg elevated, swaying her arms to the music. I giggled at the sight of the two of them.

"Where have you been all day?" My mother asked. "It's quarter after 4 already."

"Oh, just riding my bike."

"By the looks of you it was some ride. I thought that bike was too small for you," she said.

Before I could reply, Aunt Addie grabbed my hands to try to lure me into dancing with her. I did a little two-step and then broke loose to my bedroom. My aunt's powder and puff sat on the vanity, so I treated my underarms to a dusting, and then I ran a brush through my hair. I went back downstairs and started out the door to the front step.

"Oh no, you don't. Get back here to help your aunt with supper," came my mother's voice. "You've been gone all afternoon, and we need some help around here."

"But..."

"But nothing."

I rolled my eyes and followed my aunt into the kitchen.

Aunt Addie stuck her head into the refrigerator. "So, that was quite a long bike ride you had today. Did you go by yourself?"

"Yeah. Darlene and Nancy are both gone."

"It's nice to just be alone sometimes, isn't it?" My aunt pulled a package of ground beef from the refrigerator. "Here, why don't you wash your hands and shape up some hamburger patties. I'll get started on some coleslaw."

I scrubbed my hands, removed the butcher paper from the meat, and threw it into a bowl. The cool, squishy meat felt good in my hands and I played with it for a minute before I grabbed a handful, formed it into a ball, and placed a saucer across it to flatten it. "Presto! One flat burger. Works every time." I grinned at my aunt.

"You know that's not the way to flatten a hamburger, right?" said my aunt.

"That's the way Dad showed me."

"Ah, but your dad didn't learn from an expert like I did. When I was about your age I used to stop at DeCarlo's Diner each day after school for a root beer float. Every afternoon, sitting at the counter nearby was the crabbiest customer I ever knew. He used to complain to Mr. DeCarlo almost every day that there was hair in his hamburger. Mr. D. swore he used the freshest ingredients. One day he couldn't take the criticism anymore, so he decided to demonstrate to the cranky customer how he made his burgers. He placed a few ounces of hamburger in a bowl on the counter, just like you did. He sprinkled it with a little of his 'special seasoning.' The customer begged to know what was in the seasoning, but Mr. DeCarlo just smiled and said it was an old family recipe. Sure, he could tell him what it was, but then he'd have to kill him. Mr. DeCarlo then winked at me and proceeded to roll the ball into a perfect fat sphere, no edges, just like you did. And finally, Mr. DeCarlo flattened it. He picked up the rolled piece of meat and slapped it under his armpit and squeezed it shut. "And that's the way an expert makes it!"

"Eeeew! Gross! You made that up."

My aunt hooted with laughter. "I never saw that customer again," she said, "and I stuck to root beer floats." This time she couldn't stop laughing. She held her stomach and laughed and laughed until she did one of her special dances and charged up to the bathroom.

While the family sat around eating burgers that night, I ate peanut butter and jelly sandwiches instead. I begged my aunt to tell her story of how an expert made a hamburger, but she said she'd save it for another time.

CHAPTER 11

Tuesday brought a hard rain. As soon as I woke up, I looked out my bedroom window and saw Stan's car parked in front of Nancy's house. Just my luck. Stuck in the house because of the weather. The gloomy day was a perfect match for my mood and allowed me plenty of time to replay yesterday's nightmare in my mind. I spent the morning playing Crazy 8s and Parcheesi with my brothers and mother.

My mother picked up on my mood. "Is everything okay with you and the girls?"

"Yeah. It's fine. I just have some things on my mind." I gave her a weak smile.

By 11:00 am, the weather had started to clear, but Aunt Addie was still sleeping.

Mom squirmed to get comfortable. "Well, Addie went back to sleep after she took your father to work. I must be working her California body too hard. But I need some groceries in this house and that won't wait. So sweetie, I want you to run to Mead's Market and take your brothers with you to help. She held up a grocery list she had been working on between

Parcheesi moves. "I'm sure Mr. Buchanan will let you and your brothers borrow a cart to bring the groceries home."

"Aw, Mom, do Corey and Mikey have to come? The last time they came they disappeared in the toy aisle and didn't help at all, but they were sure to get a free lollipop from Mr. Buchanan when we got to the register." Michael and Corey flashed a conspiratorial smile at each other.

"Boys, you're old enough to be a help to your sister. What she says, goes." The boys nodded.

"And put your rubber boots on. There are a lot of puddles out there." The boys grinned at each other and scurried off to the cellar to find their boots.

I took the list from my mother. At least this errand would get me thinking about something else besides yesterday's disaster.

"Here's a signed check. Just fill in the amount at the register."

I opened the door just as Stan was reaching for our doorbell. He held a beautiful bouquet of summer flowers in his hand. My heart did a somersault. I gaped at him and then at the flowers. His eyes narrowed and he looked past me. "May I come in?"

"Sure." I moved aside and let him in.

He stood just inside the doorway and asked for my mother. *Oh no, he's going to tell my mother on me! She'll kill me when he tells her I was peeking in Kirby's Bar window. I have to do something about this.* "Why do you need to see my mother?"

"Because I've brought her some flowers."

"Oh...of course. She's in here," I mumbled. I led Stan into the living room to Mom.

Stan flashed one of his glamorous smiles at my mother. "Mrs. Reilly, I heard about your accident and thought you might need some cheering up. These are for you."

"Stan, how thoughtful of you, and please call me Mary. Mrs. Reilly sounds too stuffy coming from you." My mother looked over at me, and I noticed a hint of pink rise in her cheeks. She breathed in the scent of the bouquet. "Maybe I can get Bibi to place these in water for me." She handed me the flowers. "There's a vase in the top cupboard over the sink, sweetie."

I scooted into the kitchen, grateful to escape. As I arranged the bouquet in water, I strained to listen in on the conversation in the next room. I heard only dribs and drabs, but my mother's light laughter rose every now and then over Stan's mellow voice. When I determined that Stan wasn't here to rat me out, I returned to the room and placed the vase of flowers on the coffee table near my mother. Stan was seated in the chair closest to her, so I took the couch.

Stan listened intently as Mom recounted her accident to him, nodding his head at intervals and sympathizing with her, interjecting a question now and then. The conversation drifted to recounting the summer solstice party and chuckling over the silliness that had gone on. Michael and Corey finally came up from the cellar clad in their boots for the trip to the store. I had completely forgotten about the store. The boys took one look at Stan and quieted down. They looked at each other, stood at attention and saluted. Stan immediately rose to his feet and returned the favor. The boys burst into uncontrolled laughter. Stan grabbed both of them around the middle and flipped them upside-down. His well-defined muscles strained against his tee shirt.

"This is what we do to soldiers who show no respect for their commanding officers. We make them into human milkshakes." The boys yelped in laughter as Stan gave them each a hearty shake before lowering them to the ground.

"Hey, what am I missing?" Aunt Addie descended the stairs looking perfectly groomed and ready for her close-up. "When did *you* get here, soldier boy?"

"Hi, Addie." Stan took in my aunt from head to toe.

"Morning, sunshine! It's about time you got up," my mother teased.

"Well, a girl can't look that good without her beauty sleep, now can she?" Stan winked at my aunt.

My aunt's eyes lit up.

Wait a minute! You traitor! What about me? My heart ached with betrayal. *Darlene is right. He does have a thing for Aunt Addie. Who does he think he is—Mr. Charm? And look at my aunt. She's loving all the attention. What am I—chopped liver? He won't even look at me!*

Stan peeked at his watch. "Oops, I really need to get going."

"Was it something I said?" my aunt said.

"No, of course not. I promised Aunt Jean I would help her drag something out of the closet. And if I know my aunt, she'll try doing it herself and pull her back out."

"Stan, thanks again for those flowers. They really do brighten up the place," my mother chirped.

"Yeah, they do," I chimed in.

He looked directly at my mother. "My pleasure. Enjoy them and take care of yourself...Mary."

Mom blushed.

"And say 'hello' to Billy for me. Tell him I want to beat him at golf before the summer gets away from us."

"I'll do that." Mom beamed.

Aunt Addie walked over and planted herself in front of Stan. She rolled her lips into an exaggerated pout. "Just my luck. I just get here and you need to run off." She folded her arms across her chest.

"Sorry. I really need to go, but I hope I'll catch up with you at the skating party tomorrow night. You're bringing the kids, aren't you?"

The kids?? Now I'm being lumped in with the kids?

"Sure will! I wouldn't miss it." Aunt Addie smiled through her pink frosting lips. She cocked her head to one side staring at the back of Stan as he bounded out the door without as much as a glance in my direction.

"Such a nice man," my mother said. "Now about those groceries…Addie, I was going to send Bibi down to the market to pick up a few things. Do you mind driving now that you're awake?"

The reply was swift. "No. I need some breakfast. Bibi is capable of getting those groceries. I was up early enough getting Billy off to work. I can't do everything around here." She turned and headed for the kitchen.

I watched my mother's face tighten. She looked at me with hurt eyes and then looked away.

"Mom, I've already got the list and the check. I'll get the groceries." I was actually relieved not to be accompanied by my aunt. I didn't want to be around the woman who was trying to steal my man.

"Thanks, sweetie. I guess your aunt can be grumpy when she's hungry," Mom mumbled.

I shrugged, yelled for the boys to join me, and headed out the door.

Just as I knew they would, my brothers stomped their way through deep puddles as we moved down Hope Street, and then escaped to the candy aisle to search for packs of bubblegum. I didn't care. I was too involved in my own thoughts trying to make sense of the past two days. I went through the checkout and borrowed a shopping cart to carry the groceries home.

As soon as we started down the street toward home, my aunt pulled up alongside us in my father's car, smiling as if nothing had happened, there to save the day—Aunt Addie to the rescue. I gave her an exasperated sigh. She wasn't going to get off so easily this time. If she could be grumpy, so could I. She double-parked, hopped out of the car, and opened the trunk.

"Just in time," she sang out as if she was some superhero who had pulled us all from a burning building in the nick of time.

"What do you want?" I asked. " A medal, or a chest to pin it on? Oh, that's right. You have a chest. How could anyone miss it?"

My aunt glared at me.

The boys climbed into the back seat, and without a word I started loading the bags of food into the car. My aunt deserved the cold shoulder. When the cart was cleared out, I delivered it back to the market and explained to Mr. Buchanan that we didn't need it after all.

I took my time getting back to the car. Other drivers beeped at my aunt for having double parked for so long. Served her right. But to my amazement, every time someone beeped, she'd beep back, smile, and wave. When I got into the car, the only thing she said was, "Lots of friendly people in this town." I rolled my eyes and burst out laughing. Aunt Addie had won this game. But I had no intentions of letting her win the match.

CHAPTER 12

Wednesday night couldn't come soon enough. I was ready and waiting in the car at 6 o'clock sharp. All the kids in the neighborhood were sure to head up to St. Cecilia's Church parking lot for the first roller skating party of the season. My aunt borrowed my mother's skates, which in my mind, were the only professional-looking ones—white shoe skates my mother had owned since her 20s, just like the ones raffled at the end of each skating season.

Everyone who attended the St. Cecilia Summer Skate paid fifty cents to Mr. Murphy, who in exchange, gave them a raffle ticket with a number printed on it for the end of the season drawing. It was a tradition to kiss your ticket for luck and then stuff it into your sock for safe keeping.

Week after week, I squirreled away my tickets in my jewelry box and checked on my collection of numbered tickets countless times and whispered a prayer for good luck each time. The winning numbers were drawn at the last skate of the summer, and two lucky kids skated away every year with professional shoe skates with glow-in-the-dark wheels. The following season, it was evident who last summer's winners were. They coasted through the parking lot rink in front of jealous eyes. They didn't have to skate particularly well; they just had to keep from falling to look really cool.

As promised, Aunt Addie drove my brothers and me to the church skating party. At the last minute, Darlene hitched a ride with us. She hopped into the car wearing one of her carefully selected outfits for the evening. "Bibi, what do you think of my new skort?" She lifted the short skirt and showed me it had shorts underneath. "See, it's a combination of skirt and short—the newest thing. It doesn't make me look fat, does it?"

"Nope."

"Well, that's a relief. I think Joey Sobieski is going to be there and I don't want to look fat." She looked down at her legs. "This is what real skaters wear, ya know—skorts. I think it looks real professional and shows off my legs."

"Yeah, it does," I said.

Darlene was quiet for a moment. She kept eyeing her legs, and then she started again. "It doesn't make my legs look fat, does it?"

"No, it doesn't make your legs look fat. Your legs look good," I said.

She smiled. "Yeah, I do have good legs—except for one little bruise I have up here." She pointed to a tiny bruise high on her thigh. "But the skort covers that, and I don't think Joey will notice it."

"I'm sure he won't." I turned to stare out the window to give her the message that I was tired of talking about her new skort and her great legs and greasy Joey Sobieski. He used so much hair tonic that if he accidentally fell on his head (which I wasn't so sure he hadn't done already) he would just slide out of view. All I wanted to do was think of a way to make up with Stan. If I could only come up with a way to sneak off with him for a few minutes, I knew I could explain everything about Monday's date gone wrong.

It didn't take long to drive the short two miles to the church parking lot. My aunt found a parking spot on a side street. The regular parking lot had been converted into the skating rink. Two large barrels formed a barrier in front of the usual entrance to keep cars out.

Mr. Murphy stood at barrier #1 collecting the fifty cents admission from everyone and placed a lucky ticket in each hand, insisting that everyone kiss the stub for good luck. My aunt forked over two dollars to cover all of us except Darlene who had her two quarters tucked into her skort pocket. Folding chairs were set up around the parking lot perimeter for us to sit on while we slid our skates onto our shoes. I removed the string from around my neck that held my skate key, and then I cranked the clamp adjustment until my skates were locked securely into place.

Before I even had a chance to get my skates tightened, Darlene was nagging me, "Hurry up pokey, I think I see Joey."

"Wait a minute. I'm almost ready." I gave my key one final twist and stood up.

"Hey, where do you think you're going?" called my aunt. "I need some help with your brothers. You do Mikey and I'll finish Corey."

I rolled my eyes and looked at Darlene.

"Ooh, it's Joey!" she squealed. "See you out there." And she skated off.

I grappled with Mikey's skates and struggled to squish his shoes into them. The shoes were just too big for the skates to fit around. *My luck. The kid has a mutant foot.* I loosened the nut on the underside of the skate and pulled the skate's toe and heel apart to lengthen it. I slammed Mikey's shoe into the newly lengthened skate, tightened the clamps around the shoe, and then attacked the second skate. I looked up to find my aunt struggling to do the same for Corey. "Hurry up. What's taking you so long?" Mikey whined.

"Quit your belly achin', birdbrain," I muttered.

"Aunt Addie, she called me a birdbrain," Mikey wailed.

"Well, stop acting like one," my aunt scolded. Mikey went mute and gave me a hard stare.

"There, you're all set." I stood up and surveyed the parking lot. My stomach flipped when I saw Nancy and Stan paying for their tickets. My aunt finished up with Corey and proceeded to put on my mother's shoe skates. "Wait for me, you two," she called to the twins. You're going to stick near me." She looked at me. "You're free. I know you're itching to get out on the rink. Go find Darlene, and make sure she's not making a fool of herself over a boy named Joey." She winked and smiled.

I laughed and zoomed off. I sure wasn't as interested in tracking Darlene down as I was in trying to get in a moment with Stan.

The crowd had begun to thicken. I spotted Nancy doing a beeline for Darlene. Stan stood skateless and propped up against the side of the church watching as the circle of skaters floated by. It was as if he had found his private viewing station and set up to rate the skaters as they passed him. Although he was standing to my left, I had to skate almost a complete lap of the rink to get to him because Monsignor Walsh insisted the rink was "one way only…a necessary rule, my children."

This is my chance. Oh yeah, soldier boy, here I come. I zipped over and stopped sharply in front of him. He jumped a little, surprised at the sudden face-to-face.

"Hi!" I concentrated on a light and breezy tone so he knew I was in a welcoming mood and wouldn't hold a grudge. I hoped he wouldn't either.

He gave me a stern look.

"Listen Stan, I want you to know what happened and why I had to break our date."

"I don't care," he scowled. "And it wasn't a date. I don't date *children*."

My heart sank to the pit of my stomach, and I could feel my eyes well up. I fought back the tears. *I'm not going to cry. Then he'll know I'm a baby. Think fast. Say something clever to turn this around.* I looked down at the ground and felt my ears turn red. I wanted to throw my arms around his neck and cry and beg his forgiveness, just like when I was in trouble with Dad. But Stan wasn't Dad. He was a grown-up friend, and something told me I couldn't use the same tactic. After all, we were in the church parking lot surrounded by lots of people. That would not be cool.

Nothing clever came out of my mouth, nothing flirty, nothing but a small, weak "Oh."

Stan glared at me for a moment, and I watched him walk away and head straight for my aunt. She was winning, and I could do nothing about it.

CHAPTER 13

I spied on Aunt Addie from across the parking lot as she pretended not to notice Stan's approach, and watched as she went into one of her flirt routines. I saw her say something to my brothers and they skated away from her, probably pleased to be released from her watchful eyes. I watched as my aunt and Stan bantered back and forth until I couldn't take it anymore.

I skated towards the back of the church, past the large Saint Cecilia statue, and followed the path of plants and shrubs that formed a secluded labyrinth leading to the side Mary garden. Here I could be safe. Here no one would find me. I plopped myself down on the cement angel bench and started to cry just like the baby I was.

I am so stupid to think that a real grown-up would like me. His girl? Sure! The whole time he was using me to get to my aunt. Aunt Addie could have any guy she wanted. Why was she going after Stan? I hate her and I hate Stan for liking her.

Hot tears dripped down my cheeks and the sides of my nose. What a mess I had already made of my summer. I began to sob so hard that I started to hiccup. My chest heaved, and I gasped for breath. I wiped my face and nose on my sleeve and tried to pull myself together, tried to steady my breathing and stop the hiccups. It wasn't working.

Every year I looked forward to the first skating party. It was always so much fun, but this year was just complicated. Nothing was turning out right. My whole summer was turning into a disaster. Dad had lost his license for a whole month, Mom had a broken leg and wasn't any fun, my aunt was chasing my boyfriend, my boyfriend had a crush on my aunt, and no one cared that I was miserable.

"Hey." I heard a gentle voice. I looked up at the statue of the Blessed Virgin, her head bowed under a chipped blue mantle, her arms outstretched as if she were calling a player out at home plate. I hiccupped and wiped my blurry eyes. Had the Virgin spoken? I sniffed the snot back up into my nose and listened.

"I never saw you cry before." I spun around and there stood Danny Murphy peering over a tall butterfly bush.

"I'm not crying." I brushed the tears off my face and sat up straight. "And what are you spying on me for? That's pretty creepy."

"I wasn't spying on you. I was spying on him." Danny pointed to something in the bush. "Come here." He motioned me over to where he was standing.

I clomped over to him on squeaky skates.

"Quiet. Don't frighten him." Danny parted the branches of a full rhododendron. "This is Henry."

I craned my neck and squinted between thick branches into a nest that held one small, plump robin, a few fuzzy feathers scattered around him.

"Aw, isn't he cute? Hi, Henry," I whispered. "How did you know he was here?"

"Monsignor asked me if I wanted a job this summer taking care of the Mary garden. I started the end of May. That's when I discovered the nest with five robin eggs, and I've been watching them ever since."

"What happened to the others?"

"The eggs hatched and the mother bird fed the babies and taught the others to fly. The mother robin called to this one for days trying to get him to fly over to her, but he just fluttered and flopped every time. One day I decided to help him along and thought I would scare him into making his first flight."

"Oh no!"

"Yep, I shook the nest a little and out flopped Henry onto the courtyard brick. He didn't fly. He wasn't ready. I picked him up and put him back into his nest, but the mother never bothered with him after that. She flew away and left him. I've been feeding him ever since with this."

Danny turned around and grabbed a small brown lunch bag. He opened it and pulled out a jar filled with a light brown liquid, an eyedropper, and a long, slimy worm.

"Dinner time, Henry." He filled up the eyedropper. "This is bug juice. Watch. He likes it." Danny carefully touched the dropper to Henry's beak and sure enough, the bird opened his mouth and gulped the juice down. "Want to try?" He offered the eyedropper to me.

"Sure," I said. I took the dropper and mimicked what Danny had done. Henry took the juice from me with just as much enthusiasm.

"That's it. See, you can do it." He patted me on the shoulder.

I felt a lot better about things. Danny wasn't so bad after all. "Give me some more of that stuff." I plunged the eyedropper back into the solution and squeezed the tiny rubber bulb. Henry gulped the juice in his beaky birdy way.

"Okay. Don't fill him up with bug juice or he won't eat his dinner," scolded Danny. He pinched the worm, divided it into thirds, and placed one piece into the nest in front of Henry. The worm segment wiggled and looked like a mini worm. Henry eyed it, picked it up, and slurped it down. I didn't wait to be asked. I picked up another segment and placed it in front of the bird and watched him gobble that one up, too. "Henry, you're so cute!" I said.

Danny tossed the final worm installment to Henry.

"When do you think he'll fly?" I asked.

"Soon, I hope. I've been doing this for two weeks and Henry is getting fatter, but he sure isn't making an effort to fly. Soon he'll be too fat. I wish I hadn't interfered in the first place and the mother bird wouldn't have abandoned him."

I sighed. "You felt sorry for him, that's all."

"I suppose. Now I'm paying for it." He placed the eyedropper and bug juice back into the bag.

"But it's fun, right?" I said.

"Yeah, but I'm worried about him. If he doesn't fledge this week, I don't know what will happen to him when I go camping next week with my dad. Henry won't be able to get his own food if he won't leave the nest."

"I can do it for you! Really! You taught me today. You have to make up the bug juice before you go, though. I'm not squishing up any old bugs. And I know how to find worms. I've done that a million times before. I do it every time I take Mikey and Corey fishing. I'm your girl!"

Before the words even left my mouth, I felt stupid. *I'm your girl? Did I really say that?*

Danny dropped his gaze, and blushed. I wanted to crawl under the closest rosebush.

"Uh… 'ya know what I mean. I'm the person for the job. And I'll make sure the Mary garden doesn't get out of hand either."

"Great! I'll tell Monsignor you're my substitute. Thanks a lot. After all, you're pretty responsible for a cry baby," he chuckled, matching dimples appearing across his cheeks.

"Who are you calling cry baby, you creep." I poked him in the ribs and he pretended to double over in pain.

I felt my mood lighten knowing that Danny thought he could count on me. I parted the branches to peek at Henry again. His eyes were closed and his head was tucked between two little winged shoulders. "I'll take good care of you, Henry," I whispered.

Danny stood close by. Even with the extra height of my roller skates, he was still a couple inches taller than I was, but he was a couple years older. I could smell the scent from the wax he used to spike his crew cut. It smelled just like my father's. Danny looked down at me and grinned. I smiled back and then looked back at Henry. I didn't know how to end the moment, and I didn't know if I really wanted to. Suddenly, the sound of roller skates scraping along the path heading for the restrooms made the decision for me. I looked over and saw my aunt stopped along the pathway, completely unaware of Danny and me. I was still annoyed with her, so I didn't let on I was near. I watched as she rifled through her handbag and pulled out her mouthwash.

"Whoa! Look at her! That woman's drinking!' Danny pointed and started to chuckle. "I don't recognize her from church." He ducked down and spied through the branches to get a better look. "Boy, she's really scarfing it down!"

I looked at Danny and then back at my aunt who was actually gulping the stuff. "Isn't that just mouthwash?" I asked, praying that he would tell me it was.

"No, ma'am! That's the same trick my Uncle Willie uses. He tears off the label of small bottles of vodka and hides them in his sports jacket. He thinks no one knows. Mom and Dad get real sore about it." He looked at me. "I don't recognize her from church. Do you?"

I looked back at Aunt Addie. She wiped her mouth on her sleeve and twisted the top back onto the bottle and jammed it back into her purse. "No, I don't recognize her from church." It technically wasn't a lie, because my aunt didn't go to church, so how could I recognize her from church? No one would recognize her from church. As a matter of fact, I hardly recognized this woman who stood just steps away, struggling to stand up straight in my mother's skates. Aunt Addie muttered to herself as she headed back down the path toward the skating party. I looked at Danny and let out a nervous giggle.

I needed to distract him. "Okay, so it's settled. Next Monday I'll be on the job."

"You're officially hired!" He extended his hand and I shook it to seal the deal.

Danny turned to go and I took one last look at the huddled mass of feathers. "Bye, Henry. See you soon."

I scraped my way down the path towards the parking lot, while Danny walked slowly to stay even with me. We got almost to the end of the path when we came face-to-face with Stan. Stan took one look at me and then narrowed his eyes on Danny. I didn't say anything. I wanted to tell him about Henry and my new job. I wanted to take his hand and lead him to the garden and show him the tiny bird. I wanted to see him smile at me and call me his girl. Instead, his gaze hardened, and he put his head down and stormed by me.

CHAPTER 14

Darkness descended on the parking lot and the floodlights came on. Carnival-like music blasted above the rumble of skates and the laughter and chatter of the crowd. At exactly 8:00 pm came the announcement "adult skate only," and all the kids cleared the parking lot. I watched my aunt and prayed she would stay put and not venture out onto the lot. But that was not to be. She wobbled into the rink and almost crashed into Gary Trowbridge's dad. She barely missed Mrs. Murphy and wasn't so lucky with Mrs. Polansky. The poor rotund lady flew off the concrete into the grass, her skirt flying up into the air. She landed on her knees and slid about three feet before stopping in front of Stan who ran to help her up and dust her off.

Aunt Addie zoomed by giving fake locomotive toots to warn people to get out of her way, whooping and giggling as she swerved in front of Stan who grabbed her hand and pulled her over to the side of the rink. "Slow down there, cowgirl!" he hollered.

My aunt threw his hand off and started howling with laughter. "Did you see me? I'm a skating whiz! Here, just watch me!" She took off again before Stan could catch her and did another clumsy whirl around the rink. "Watch out for the Roller Derby Queen!" she hooted. She elbowed Monsignor Walsh as she passed him. The next time she came around in front of Stan, he grabbed her more forcefully and ushered her away from the crowd. I couldn't hear what he said to her, but I could see from her reaction she didn't like it one bit. My aunt stomped over to a nearby bench and plunked herself down. Stan walked away shaking his head.

Adult skate time continued for two more long songs. Darlene and Nancy stood off to the side. I caught them whispering and staring at my aunt. I wanted to die. I searched for Danny to see how he was reacting but couldn't find him. It looked like he had gone home.

Adult skate time ended, and things returned to normal. I breathed a sigh of relief when I saw my aunt remove her skates and shuffle down towards the bathroom again. I watched her pull her bottle of clear liquid out of her purse, finish off the contents, and throw it into the trash. It made me feel sad and creepy inside. I realized Danny was right about her.

At five minutes before nine, Mr. Murphy announced skating was about to end, so everybody could get one last skate in. Kids and parents charged onto the rink for a few more turns, showing off moves they had perfected over the course of the night. Then the lights flickered, and people removed their skates, left the lot, and trudged to their cars.

I found Michael and Corey and helped them yank off their skates. The place was pretty much cleared out and still there was no sign of Aunt Addie. I told my brothers to sit on one of the benches and stay and wait for me while I checked out the bathroom. I darted down the path and stopped short when I heard someone crying in the Mary garden. I peeked over the bushes, and sure enough, there sat my aunt, head in her hands, crying her eyes out as if she had just heard both her cats were dead.

I cleared my throat and walked in between the bushes. "Um... Aunt Addie? Is everything okay?"

She started. "What d'ya want? Leave me alone!"

"What's wrong? Why are you crying?" I asked.

"It's none of your business. Go back to your skating."

"Skating's over. Almost everyone left already."

"Oh, well why didn't ya say so. Let's get outta here. Where're your brothers?" She stood on wobbly legs.

I gulped and took a deep breath. "Aunt Addie, are you... uh...drunk?"

"No I'm not drunk, you stupid girl! Who have you been talkin' to? What did he tell you? That stupid man!"

Man?? Danny's only a teenager!

"For your information..." I looked at her disheveled hair, red nose, and raccoon eyes. "Oh never mind."

This was not my aunt talking. Why was she so much fun one minute and so crabby the next? After tonight I guess I knew the answer to that. I looked at my beautiful aunt stumbling and mumbling, and I felt my heart crumble. I had believed her when she said that bottle she carried around with her was mouthwash. She's right. I am stupid. "Come on, Aunt Addie." I took her hand and she steadied herself a little. "Let's go."

"Now... where are my... keys? Those darn keys." My aunt fumbled through her purse. *Oh no! She can't drive Dad's car like this! How long does it take someone to sober up?*

We plowed our way down the path and found Darlene pacing next to my brothers. "Where have you been?" Darlene stared at my aunt and then turned to me. Her eyes got big. Then she turned back to my aunt. "Stan asked me if I wanted to ride home with him to keep him company, Miss Treat. Nancy's father brought Mrs. Polansky and Nancy home earlier after you…" She stopped herself. "I mean, after she fell."

"Poor Stan needs some company. Waa, waa." My aunt rubbed her balled fists over her eyes like a crybaby. She started to weave and then stumbled.

Michael and Corey looked at each other and started jumping up and down. "We want to drive with Stan, too! We want to drive with Stan!"

My aunt puffed out her chest and blurted, "None of you are ridin' home with that creep! You came with me and you're goin' home with me!" Her eyes were wild and unfocused. "And that's f-f-f-inal! That man needs to get some friends his own age!"

Stan appeared out of the shadows just in time to hear my aunt's outburst. Seeing him inflamed her more. "Who are you, the pied piper? All the kids in town want to hang around with Stan. Isn't he wonderful?" She stretched her arms out wide and stumbled." Everyone loves a man in uniform, now don't they? And soldier boy loves all of them, too!"

Stan's eyebrows shot up and I saw his eyes flash. "By the looks of it Addie, *everyone*, including you, should be driving home with me."

The color in my aunt's cheeks rose. She did a sloppy march over to him and placed one hand on her hip. The other wagged the car keys in front of his nose. "Listen up, sold…jer… boy." She swayed. "These kids came with me…and…they're goin' home with me." She punctuated each sentence with a poke at his chest. "And…and you can take that back to your barracks!" Then Aunt Addie flew into a fit of laughter, staggered over to the bench, and plopped herself down, pointing and giggling at the storm crossing Stan's face.

Without a word, Stan walked over and removed the keys from my aunt's hand and placed them in mine. "Bibi, help me get Addie into your father's car. Darlene, take the boys to my car and wait for me."

Darlene and the boys took off. Stan and I each took an arm and shuffled my aunt into the back seat of our car. All the while she was muttering, "And you can take that back to your barracks...and you can take that back to your barracks," giggling each time she said it.

Stan told me to get in the passenger side and lock the doors while he took the others home and went to get my father.

"But my father..."

"I know. He lost his license. Everyone's figured that out. Under the circumstances, I think your father would rather drive his own car home. I'll follow him, and if he gets stopped I'll explain to the police what happened." Then Stan did the strangest thing. He bent over and stroked my face. "Hey, I'm sorry."

I gave him a weak smile. Was Stan sorry about my aunt making a fool out of herself, or sorry about how he had acted with me? I didn't know what to think. Maybe this was the way grown up love was, never knowing, never feeling sure, never understanding.

By the time Stan left, Aunt Addie was already snoring in the backseat. I sat in the car and waited. The floodlight that illuminated the parking lot snapped off from inside the rectory.

Sitting in the car in the dark waiting for my father gave me a chance to puzzle over the night's happenings. Stan had come to our rescue. He had been so kind and understanding, so different from the way he was acting earlier.

Is this all part of being a teenager? One minute someone seems to like you, and the next minute they don't want you around? Mom and Dad aren't like that. Why are Stan and Aunt Addie that way, and why do I still care so much about both of them in spite of it?

It wasn't long before my father arrived to retrieve us. He thanked Stan and didn't say anything to me all the way home. Was he just thinking? Was he nervous about a policeman catching him driving? Or was my father mad at me, too, for letting this happen?

CHAPTER 15

The next few days were filled with tension at our house. I continually interrupted serious discussions between my parents and my aunt, and I was sure my parents were going to send her packing back to California. Actually, I couldn't help wishing for just that.

For three nights I awoke to sniffling from the bed next to me. These times I didn't rush over to my aunt's bed and offer to rub her back to relax her. Instead I just lay there, still angry with her, listening to her suffer.

The peculiar odor in my bedroom of stale pot pourri gradually disappeared. My mother was now able to climb stairs slowly, and she was once again making her presence known on the second floor. Aunt Addie worked outside quite a bit in the yard and started a little herb garden. She spent her days tidying the yard, sunning herself in the hammock, and taking long walks.

Before Danny left on his fishing trip, he dropped off a bucket of worms, a jar of bug juice, and an eyedropper for me to help feed Henry. He gave me some final feeding and gardening tips and wished me luck. Every morning I looked forward to hopping on my bicycle and pedaling to the church to take care of my responsibilities. Caring for Henry and tending the Mary garden provided a good escape for me.

Afternoons, Mom routinely asked me to walk down to the market for dinner supplies. Aunt Addie offered to help once in a while, but I refused the help. Table conversations were polite, but no one got silly the way we used to. My aunt and mother no longer lingered over a glass of wine after dinner.

Dad's car stood unused at the top of the driveway. He started it up every couple of days to make sure the battery didn't die on him. Stan had come to the rescue, driving my father to work each morning and bringing him home at night. Some days Dad would convince him to come in for an iced tea after work, and they'd talk Yankees and golf.

The 4th of July came and went without much fanfare. Fireworks at Cummings Park were just ho-hum. And Stan went back to ignoring me again.

The strangest thing happened on the second Wednesday afternoon following "the incident." My aunt went out for one of her walks and met up with Stan. I saw the two of them sauntering down the street, and they seemed to be having a serious but friendly discussion. That night after supper, Aunt Addie announced that she would be going out with Stan for the evening. My heart sank.

When she returned a couple hours later, Stan walked her to the door. I was spying on them from my bedroom window, craning my neck to listen in to their conversation. He squeezed her hand and flashed his smile. "So, same time next week?"

She nodded a 'yes.'

It took a couple of weeks, but the mood among the adults started to lift. When Stan wasn't taxiing my father back and forth to work, or dating my aunt, or ignoring me, he was over at the Kennedys' house.

Every time I'd see Darlene she gushed over Stan and something cute he had said or done. Joey Sobieski was a forgotten flame. And she wasn't a bit threatened by the tight little relationship Stan had with my aunt. Darlene was convinced Stan had a crush on *her* instead. She never was one to lack confidence.

I tried to match Darlene's stories by fabricating "special little moments" I had shared with Stan at our house when he brought my father home from work. I told her some nights he stayed for dinner, and he pushed in my chair at the dinner table. I told her how we clowned around while we did the dishes together. I even told her a joke he had told me—one that I had actually heard my father tell. I was so convincing that even *I* was beginning to believe myself.

One day I saw Darlene get out of Stan's car with a big grin pasted across her face. She stood in the street waving goodbye to him smiling, completely oblivious to the fact that I was moping on my front step. I watched her drool after him as his car slowly rolled past my house down the three houses to Nancy's house. He looked my way briefly as he passed me and smirked. Darlene skipped up to her front door and ran inside. She didn't even hear me when I called her name. I bolted over to her house and knocked on the door. When she answered, she was radiant.

"Come in. I have the best news!" She yanked me across the threshold. "Let's go up to my room so nobody hears." She cocked her head and rolled her eyes to signal her mother was in the kitchen. As we scampered up the stairs, she yelled, "Ma, I'm home!" We barely heard Mrs. Kennedy's reply.

"So, tell me." I waited. *Do I really want to hear another Darlene and Stan story? Can I bear it?*

She started giggling. "I was coming back from Bongo's and Stan came by and asked me if I wanted a ride home. So I jumped in, just like that. His car smells so good and it's sooo luxurious. I felt like Doris Day with Rock Hudson. Stan had on some music station that my father listens to, but I didn't mind. When I told him I loved his car, he asked me if I wanted to take a little spin. Me! He wanted to take me for a little spin. Ooh! 'Of course, silly,' I said. So instead of coming home, he turned the car around and we drove around for a little while."

Darlene paused. "You are not going to believe what he said next." She touched her face. "He said he liked my cheekbones, and he would sure like to sketch me sometime! Sketch me! And my cheekbones!"

"Oh, he told me that, too." *That'll give you something to think about!*

Darlene shot me a dismissive look and strolled to the mirror to examine her face, turning her head from side to side so she could drink in her bone structure. "I can't stand it. I think he really likes me. You know, I don't think he's interested in your aunt at all, especially after the skating party." Darlene paused and gave me one of her I-feel-sorry-for-you stares.

She looked back in the mirror. "Ya know I do look older than I am. I think I'm going to start wearing more makeup." She hesitated. "And Stan did say something else right before he dropped me off, but I can't tell you that. He asked that it just be our *special secret*." She smirked.

That's just great. Blabbermouth Darlene, who could never keep any of the secrets I shared with her over the years, all of a sudden is into keeping secrets? Darlene and her high cheekbones are going to get sketched. And she really will get it done. There won't be any complications in her life involving a mother with a broken leg. I wonder if Stan called her "his girl." That's probably the little morsel she's keeping from me, her best friend.

Suddenly I felt sick to my stomach. "Well, I can't stay long. I'm going to need to run down to the market for my mother." I couldn't resist saying what I said next, even though I felt devious saying it. "I think your idea of wearing a lot more makeup is a really good one, Dar. I think it will make you look older and guys sure like makeup." I smiled, showed myself to the door, and yelled a goodbye to Mrs. Kennedy. I ran out the front door and across the street. *Oh yeah, Stan will really like you in a lot of makeup, you traitor!*

The next day Nancy announced to Darlene and me that she and her parents were taking off to spend two weeks in Lake George. Stan was staying behind to house sit and looking forward to having the house to himself for his "bachelor pad." I wondered what kind of entertaining a bachelor would do. Come to think of it, I had never seen any other bachelors come to visit him. This could be interesting.

While Darlene concentrated on experimenting with makeup, I concentrated on looking for an opportunity to get a certain bachelor alone to plead my case. I still owed him an explanation of why I didn't show up to sit for his sketching session. I had to talk to him or I would die. My opportunity came the following morning at about ten o'clock.

CHAPTER 16

I watched from my bedroom window as Nancy and her parents and Stan jam-packed their family wooden-sided Ford station wagon with floats and coolers and luggage. I was excited for Nancy because the Polanskys usually didn't go anywhere. But I was more excited for me because now Stan would be alone. It would be easier for me to make contact with him. I was on high alert. No time like the present, I thought. I bounded down the stairs to the basement and found my roller skates. I flung them over my shoulder and tromped out to the front steps to strap them on. Just as the Polanskys got into their car, I went whizzing down the sidewalk to bid a last farewell to my-good-friend-who-I-would-miss-so-much-and-I-hoped-would-have-a-wonderful -vacation. I gushed so much that I sounded phony even to myself.

Stan gave me an odd look as I squeezed Nancy's hand one more time through her open car window and pressed a quarter into her palm pleading with her to "send me a postcard or two." I felt like a needy grandmother sending her first grandchild off to camp for the first time. Nancy's face lit up and she promised me she would.

Stan reached out and touched Nancy's hand and smiled. "Can't wait 'til you get back, cuz." Nancy pulled her hand away and stared into her lap. I stood close to Stan and we waved goodbye to them until the car disappeared down the street.

As soon as they were gone, I turned to Stan. "So I guess you'll be a bachelor for a while?"

"Yeah. Well, see ya." He turned toward the house.

I knew I had to say what was on my mind now, or I would miss my chance. "Stan, look. I'm really sorry about not showing up for our sketching date. It's not that I didn't try. That was the morning my father had his court appearance and my aunt had to drive him. I was stuck home with Mom and her broken leg. By the time I could break free, you were already gone."

"You already told me this. I waited for over an hour for you at that spot. I packed a picnic and everything. I guess I'm just not that important to you." He looked down at the ground and ran his fingers over his blonde crew cut.

"But you *are* important to me. *Real* important. I drove my bike all over town looking for you until I found you at Kirby's. Why didn't you come out to talk to me? I know you saw me through the window. Why didn't you let on you knew me?" I waited for him to look up.

"Look. I was real mad. I needed to cool off."

"Well, you cooled off, okay. You've hardly spoken to me since that day. I thought I was your girl."

"My girl? By the looks of it, *my girl* didn't waste any time finding someone else at the skating party." He crossed his arms in front of his chest and looked away again.

"Danny? You think I like Danny? You're all wrong. I'm doing a job for Danny while he's on vacation."

"A job? What kind of a job?"

"I'm feeding a bird for him and taking care of the church's Mary garden. That's where we were coming from the other night when you passed us. Danny was explaining to me what needed to be done for Henry." (Of course, I wasn't going to tell Stan that Danny had found me bawling my eyes out over him).

"Slow down. Who's Henry?"

I laughed. "Don't worry. He's not another boy. Henry's a baby robin whose mother abandoned him. It's a long story. But Danny feels responsible, so he's been feeding Henry until he can fly on his own. And Danny's been keeping the Mary garden trimmed for Monsignor. While he's on vacation, I offered to take over for him."

Stan didn't say anything.

"And since we're asking questions, why have you been getting so chummy with my aunt?" I blurted out. There, I said it and couldn't take it back.

"Chummy with your aunt?" He laughed and narrowed his eyes on me. "You're jealous, aren't you?"

"Me? Jealous? No, I don't care."

"I think you do."

"I do not!" It was my turn to fold my arms across my chest. "Besides, look who's talking about being jealous. You're the one who got bent out of shape over Danny!"

He stared at me for what seemed like forever.

My heart sank. "I thought so. You do like my aunt. You've been meeting up with her on her walks and you've been taking her out on dates. 'Same time next week, Addie?' I thought you were mad at her for getting drunk. And what about Darlene? 'Oh, Darlene, you have such great cheekbones. I need to sketch them.'"

Stan's eyes lit up in a mocking smile. "Have you been spying on me?"

"Spying! Huh! You don't need to be a spy to see what's going on. I'm not dumb ya know."

"Bibi, I don't think you're dumb. I just think you're confused. First of all, your aunt needs someone to like her right now, because she sure doesn't like herself. She feels she's embarrassed her family and made a fool of herself in front of the whole neighborhood."

"Then why doesn't she just go back to California where she belongs."

"Because she's hurting too much right now to go home. She needs her family, and that includes you, to help get her through this. As for our Wednesday night dates as you call them, I'll leave that up to your aunt to tell you about."

I couldn't think of anything to say. I felt ashamed for wishing that my aunt would just leave, but I still didn't approve of the Wednesday night dates.

"And as for Darlene," Stan continued. "Darlene is the opposite of your aunt. She likes herself *too* much. She begged *me* to sketch her."

I knew it! Darlene made the whole thing up! I wonder what other lies she told me. "I need to sketch Darlene because she made me promise, but I'd rather sketch a girl as pretty as you if you'd only give me another chance."

He smiled and I felt my belly tighten.

"You mean it?" I gulped.

"Sure I do. And now that I have the house to myself this week, I can set up my studio there. We won't have to meet in the woods. I could do it as a surprise for your parents for being so nice to me this summer. We could keep it a secret from them until it's done."

I couldn't believe my ears. Stan was giving me a second chance. He was giving *us* a second chance. And together we would surprise my parents.

"When? When?" I yelped. "I think we should set it up as soon as possible. I'm available tomorrow!"

"Well, unfortunately, tomorrow is the day I said I would sketch Darlene."

"Oh." I hated the idea that Darlene was going to be sketched before me.

"How about the next day? Come around noon and I'll make lunch for us and then we'll have our session."

"Sure!" See you Friday at noon." I glided off on my skates, did a twirl in the street, and yelled back to him. "It's a date!"

Stan grinned back and watched me until I got to my house. We waved to each other before he walked into the Polanskys' house. I sat down on my front porch to remove my skates but quickly decided against it. This was a skating day, no doubt about it. I felt lighter than I had in weeks and nothing could dampen my mood. I sailed down the street twirling and skating on one foot and humming, congratulating myself for speaking up and making things right between my boyfriend and me. Yes, things were working out after all. I thought I would burst. I had a sketching date with Stan.

CHAPTER 17

I got up early and zoomed to feed Henry before I had break-fast. Baby birds needed a lot of attention and a lot of food I was beginning to realize. Every couple of hours seemed to be the norm.

Just before noon, Darlene showed up at my house. Without being asked, she scampered up the stairs to my room with me close behind her. As soon as we reached my bedroom, she closed and locked the door so that we could have some privacy.

"What are you doing here? I thought today was your sketch-ing session with Stan?"

"Exactly! But I did something stupid. I told my mother about it, and she said that if Stan wanted to sketch me, he could do it at our house. We just had a big blow up, and I told her I was coming over here. I knew she watched me come over here. I needed it to look that way. I'm actually going to sneak out the back way, cut through a few backyards, and double back to the woods. I can't disappoint him. So you're my alibi."

I made a mental note that Stan had not offered to meet her at his bachelor pad. It made me feel more special. "I don't know about this, Darlene. I don't want to lie to your mom."

"Oh, don't be so immature. Besides, you won't have to lie to her. She saw me come over here, and this is where she'll think I am. But I need a favor before I go. Where's that cute peasant blouse of yours? I want to borrow it."

Oh no! Not the blouse that Stan liked so much! I was going to wear that for my sketching date. No way! I'm not loaning it to her.

"Sorry. It's in the wash."

"Darn! I had my heart set on that. What else do you have?"

Darlene darted over to my dresser and started rifling through my drawers. She held up shirt after shirt, and discarded item after item across my bed, giving much of my meager wardrobe the hairy eyeball, commenting on each piece. "No…no… yuck! I thought you got rid of this a long time ago." Then she spotted it—my orange-flowered halter top. Her eyes widened.

"Where did *you* get this?" she squealed.

Before I could answer, she lifted her shirt over her head and squeezed into the halter top. Her large breasts spilled over. It sure looked different on Darlene than it did on me. She ran over to check her reflection in my mirror and twirled herself around. "When did *your* mother let you buy this?"

"Actually, my mother didn't. My aunt brought it for me from California. My mother won't let me wear it."

"Oh, that makes sense." Darlene gave herself another once over and smiled at what she saw. "Your aunt is so cool. This is perfect. Now all I need is a little makeup."

"Here." I handed her my peach blush with the tiny brush that came in the compact.

Her face screwed up. "Is this all you have?"

"Well, yeah. I think I have some Vaseline you can put on your lips.

Darlene snorted. "Are you kidding? Hey, what's that?" Her eyes lit on my aunt's little makeup bag. Before I could speak, she was opening the bag and inspecting the bottles and tubes of color.

"I don't think you should be touching that stuff."

"Don't be silly. Your aunt's cool. She appreciates the tools of beauty."

I watched as Darlene made her selections. She applied frosted coral lipstick, two thick stripes of blue and purple eye shadow, black eyeliner and deep plum rouge. "How do I look?" she asked.

Darlene's face was a parade of color carrying two fleshy balloons under her neck. I couldn't keep from smiling. "Perfect! Very sophisticated. Stan will love it."

"I think so, too. One more thing." She grabbed my comb and teased a clump of hair into a little nest on the top of her head. She then pulled her own shirt back on to cover the halter top while she escaped. "Okay, wish me luck."

I went downstairs first to see where my mother and aunt were. They were sunning themselves in the backyard, yakking away. I waved Darlene on when the coast was clear and sent her out the side kitchen door. After that, she was on her own. I watched her throw her bag over the fence, hop it, and slink away. She never once turned back or looked over her shoulder.

I peered out the window at my mother and aunt, still sun-bathing in the only two chaise lounges we owned, their bodies stretched out in the sun, glasses of lemonade in their hands. My aunt, sporting a hot pink two-piece, was slicked with a solution of baby oil and iodine and held a reflective cardboard to her chest. Mom, in her sensible navy one piece, wore dark glasses and a large brimmed straw hat with Florida printed across it in big green palm tree letters, a souvenir Mrs. Kennedy had brought back to her from one of their many trips.

I remembered what Stan had said about Aunt Addie needing a friend and not liking herself. How could she not like herself? She looked amazing! But why the big secret about Wednesday nights? I needed to do some super sleuthing, and now seemed the right time. I slipped into my bathing suit, grabbed a beach towel out of the linen closet, poured myself some lemonade, and went outside to join the ladies.

"Hi, cupcake!" my aunt greeted me as I spread the beach towel out.

I plopped myself down on the towel. "Hi."

"Coming out to soak up some rays with us?" asked Mom. And before I could answer she added, "Where are the girls today?"

"Nancy left on vacation and Darlene…well, she had some sort of an appointment."

"Where are the boys?" I asked.

"Oh, your brothers went over to Nelson's house. Stevie got a guinea pig and he promised to let them hold it. That's why it's so quiet around here and why Addie and I are catching some rays."

I smiled. "So… speaking of 'Where the Boys are,'… that movie starts at the State Theater this week. Maybe we girls could go to the opening show *Wednesday* night?" I waited.

My mother and aunt looked at each other, and then my aunt shifted in her lounge chair, closed her eyes, and got quiet.

Mom straightened. "A movie sounds like a great idea. Let's go during the day and we'll go to 'Swiss Family Robinson' so that the boys can come, too. That's something we'll all enjoy!"

"But I've heard so much about the other one! Connie Francis sings in it. You love her! Besides, 'Swiss Family Robinson' is for babies. I don't want to go to a baby movie."

"Well, what I've heard about 'Where the Boys Are' is that it's not a movie for a young girl either. There's some suggestive content in it."

"What's digestive content?" I asked.

My aunt snorted. "Yeah, Mary, what's digestive content?"

It was my mother's turn to laugh. "*Suggestive* content means there's stuff in it that's not appropriate for my daughter. Let's just leave it at that." She stood up. "My skin is starting to cook. I'm going inside." She gathered up her lemonade and mopped her forehead with her forearm. "And time to turn so you don't burn, Addie."

My aunt rolled her eyes and turned onto her stomach. She unlatched her bathing suit top. "Will you rub some of this stuff on my back and legs, sweet cheeks?" She offered up the bottle of homemade tanning solution.

My turn to roll my eyes. "I guess." I tromped over to her lounge chair and bent over while she trickled the oil onto my palm. I began rubbing it onto her back.

"Make sure it covers evenly. I want my tan to be perfect, ya know."

I rolled my eyes again. I don't know who I was rolling them at, actually, but it did make me feel better.

"When you finish my back, do the back of my legs, too, please."

Who does she think I am? Her servant? "Keep it even. Do my legs."

I looked at the oil. "Don't you think this stuff will cook your skin?"

"That's what it's supposed to do. Pretty soon I'll be a rich, glamorous bronze."

"It looks like you'll go through the red, pimply stage first." My eyes scanned the red rash across her shoulders and the back of her legs.

"Well, beauty has its sacrifices," she said.

Okay. I have to get back on track here. Wednesday night. Wednesday night.

"So, maybe you and I can go to that movie on Wednesday night, because I'm pretty mature for my age."

"Even if your mother would let you go, which she won't, I have another engagement that night."

"What other engagement?"

"Just some place I need to be."

No! That's not going to happen. She's not getting off so easy. I'm not going to politely go away.

"Where do you need to be that's more important than a night out with your admiring niece?"

I need to go somewhere that's very important to me right now. I'll just leave it at that."

"Because you're going out with Stan! That's why! That's who is more important than me. You think I don't know you like him. Well, sorry, but I don't think he likes you as much as you think he does. I'll tell you that right now. I think he only takes you out on Wednesdays because he feels sorry for you!"

My aunt clipped the back of her bathing suit and rolled over. She sat up and stared at me for a long time. Her eyes got very sad. I could feel my face redden, and I felt ashamed of the words that had just escaped my lips. But there was no taking them back.

"So, this is what it's all about? You have a crush on Stan, and you think I'm taking him away from you?"

I looked down at my oily hands.

"I'm not going anywhere with Stan this Wednesday night," she said.

"You're not?"

"No. I can go alone now." Her eyes brimmed with tears. "Stan was good enough to take me to my first two AA meetings. From now on, I'll go alone."

I searched my aunt's face. "AA meetings? That's for alcoholics, isn't it?"

"Yes, it is." She squirmed and looked down at her sunburned legs. "Your good ole Aunt Addie has a drinking problem." She gave a weak smile.

I shut up and stared at her. How could I have been so stupid? The fake mouthwash…the smelly bedroom…the mood swings… the incident at the skating party… the hushed conversations around the house. Stan's words came flying back to me. *"She's hurting too much right now to go home. She needs her family, and that includes you, to help get her through this."*

There was an awkward silence while my aunt waited for me to say something. She finally spoke. "I can see from the look on your face that you don't believe me. You're thinking Aunt Addie can't have a drinking problem. She still looks like the same person she always was."

"I…I guess I didn't know. I thought maybe the skating night was just a one-time thing. I'm sorry I said those mean things. I didn't understand…" I rushed into her arms and held her tight. I didn't care that she was covered in grease and that she had sweaty armpits. I didn't care that her arms were sunburned and pimply. There was no place else I wanted to be. My aunt needed me and I was sure going to be there. My eyes welled up. I guess I wasn't so mature for a thirteen-year-old after all.

"Of course, you didn't know, honey. That's what's so unique about alcoholics. We're clever when it comes to denying it and hiding it for long periods of time. Then one day it just gets out of hand and others start to notice. The worst of it comes when we see ourselves for what we really are. Both things happened to me at the same time at the skating party. I'm pretty thankful that Stan didn't let you and your brothers get in the car with me. You don't have to worry. Stan isn't romantically attracted to me, sweetie. I'm not sure what interests him, actually. He's a hard one to figure out."

She took my shoulders and pushed me back to look into my eyes. I quickly brushed the tears away. "I can see you and your girlfriends have crushes on Stan and think he's a real cute soldier. Just remember, he's dreamy to look at, but he's too old for you, and at the end of the summer he'll be gone, probably breaking hearts somewhere else. It's what gorgeous men like that do. And I don't want my favorite niece to have her heart broken, okay?"

I giggled. "Your favorite niece? I'm your *only* niece."

"See! I might be a drunk, but I'm honest as the day is long!" She chuckled and swatted me across the rump. "Okay, let me get up. I'm fried."

I gave her another hug. "I love you, Aunt Addie…and you're my favorite aunt." I gave her a smirk.

She laughed. "Touché! Now I need to shower this grease off, and then I promised your mother I'd cut back that hydrangea bush for her."

"Oh no! I forgot the Mary garden and Henry! I'm late. Gotta go."

I grabbed Henry's bug juice, hopped on my bicycle, and pumped my way up the hill to the church.

CHAPTER 18

By the time I got to the church, it was well past noon. Danny had told me the next feeding time should be at 10:30 am. "One feeding early in the morning, and then he's hungry again at 10:30. Don't let him go much later than that, or he'll start chirping up a racket and draw the attention of other animals."

I skidded down the path and stopped short in front of Henry's bush. "I'm here, Henry," I sang out. I filled the dropper with bug juice and carefully parted the branches in front of his nest. There lay the nest, empty except for a few short downy feathers. My heart raced. *Oh no! Henry! Where are you?* I dug through the bushes looking for him. No Henry. I looked all around on the ground beneath the bushes in case he had fallen. No Henry. "Henry! Henry! Where are you?" I yelled.

I sat down on the garden bench holding my head in my hands. Just then, Franklin, Monsignor Walsh's tabby darted out from under the bench and scampered across my feet. Startled, I remembered Danny's warning, "...*he'll draw the attention of other animals.*"

"Franklin, stop!" The cat turned around and looked at me through sleepy green eyes. "What did you do to Henry?" I envisioned the gory scene that must have taken place, the shadow of a long, hungry, furry claw stretching across Henry's nest. The possibilities were too frightening. I started after the cat, but he quickly scampered away and ran for cover under the lattice-protected porch of the church rectory.

I can't even do a simple job for a friend. I'm useless. What will I tell Danny when he returns? How can I face him? Yeah, I'm the girl for the job all right. Just leave it to me. I'll get your bird killed. Danny trusted me to take good care of Henry, and I let him down. I'm so tired of letting people down. I can't do anything right.

I flopped back down on the bench and flung the bug juice and the eyedropper to the ground. My throat tightened in self-pity. I felt tears prick at the backs of my eyes and blur my vision. Then I heard it. Soft at first, then louder, and again still louder. Chirping came from between the bushes, and a flurry of feathers dove at the bug juice splattered across the ground. One...two...three...four hungry robins landed just feet from where I sat. Keeping their yellow eyes fastened on me, they pecked at the ground scavenging for the remains of the juice.

I grabbed the discarded jar and poured all the juice that I could salvage onto a leaf and stepped away to allow the birds to feed. They chirped with excitement, spreading the word of the free lunch. Five...six. Two more charged in, and there, smack in the middle of the feeding frenzy stood the fattest and hungriest of them all. A small gold mark under his beak glinted in the afternoon sunlight as he threw back his throat to guzzle down the bug juice. I began to laugh. Henry had brought the whole family to dine, and Henry had learned to fly.

"You big, fat, ball of feathers. You almost gave me a heart attack." I smiled as I watched the juice disappearing, some of it being gobbled up by the small flock and the rest of it seeping into the garden soil.

"So, how long have you known how to fly? Have you been using Danny and me to do your bug hunting and feeding? Maybe you're more clever than we gave you credit for. That's it for you. You fend for yourself from now on—and watch out for Franklin. He looks like he'd enjoy getting his claws on a fat, unsuspecting *candy bar* like you." I smiled at the bird. "Oh Henry, it's so good to see you." I felt my heart brimming with joy and pride. Henry had taken his first flight, and it had happened on my watch. I couldn't wait to tell Danny.

I quickly pinched off faded blossoms and watered the garden, said a quick Hail Mary in front of the Blessed Virgin, and hopped on my bicycle. Darlene should be back from her sketching session by now and I wanted to hear all about it. I felt so good, I'd even let her brag a little about it.

I went straight to Darlene's house. A note was taped to the door in Mrs. Kennedy's handwriting.

Darlene, I've run to the store for a few things for supper. Stay at Bibi's until I get back. Be back soon. Mom

Uh oh, I gulped. Mrs. Kennedy thought Darlene was still at our house. Speaking of Darlene...I couldn't believe she wasn't back yet. The suspense was killing me. I went home and clamped on my roller skates, giving them an extra twist with my skate key. I slipped the key on the twine over my head and around my neck and took off. Maybe skating would relax me a little.

After five minutes of practicing twirls and jumps and skating backwards, I had a sneaky idea. What Darlene didn't know wouldn't hurt her. Maybe I could do a little bit of spying on her session, just to see what it would be like for me. And I knew the perfect spot to do it.

I skated up Harmonica Hill behind the woods. There was a narrow path that entered the clearing from the other side. We kids rarely used it because Old Lady Brown didn't like us anywhere near her property. Once, Jimmy Springer swore he saw a shotgun peering out her kitchen window. He claimed she patrolled for bad kids all the time.

As I approached the path, I spied the back of Stan's red Bonneville pulled off the road into the bushes. An eagle bumper sticker with *U.S. Army* printed across it peeked out between the leaves. *That's odd. Why did Stan drive here instead of just walking through the path to the woods?*

I took off my skates, laid them at the end of the path, and walked over to the car. It was empty. I peeked inside the windows and scanned the front seat, recalling the leather smells and jazzy music the day Stan had taken me for my magical spin. An old *Stamford Advocate* lay on the passenger side. The image of that missing girl's face smiled up at me. I figured Stan must be pretty upset about it to have kept that newspaper.

As I started down the path, I noticed a piece of blue and white striped cloth hanging out of the trunk of the car. It looked like a towel. I smiled as I wondered how long Stan had been driving around with his beach towel hanging out of his trunk. He'd be embarrassed when he discovered it. I could just tuck it back inside for him and he wouldn't even know. I grabbed the handle to the trunk and yanked. It was locked. Oh well.

I started to walk away and then remembered that my father's car had a little lever somewhere near the driver's seat that he pulled when he wanted to open the trunk. I wondered if Stan's car had the same setup. I pulled on the driver's door handle, and the door opened. I sat behind the large wheel and searched for the lever like I had seen my father do. I leaned down under the steering wheel and looked around. Part of me felt like a trespasser, but part of me enjoyed sitting behind the wheel and doing something important for Stan that would save him an embarrassing moment.

Will I eventually tell him what I did, or should I keep it a secret from him? Maybe I'll slip it into conversation and tease him about it during my sketching session? I liked the idea of having something to tease him about. It felt like a grown-up, flirty thing to do in a relationship. Then I spotted them. Two little pull levers with symbols above them that looked like the ones in my father's car. Eeny-meeny-miney-mo. I pulled the lever closest to me and ...click! The hood of the car popped up slightly. *Oh no! Wrong choice, you ninny!*

I raced around to the front of the car and pressed the hood back down into place. My eyes stole looks down the path, nervous that Stan would hear me messing with his car. Maybe this wasn't such a great idea after all. I stood there for a minute until my heart calmed down. *Well, I guess I know what lever to pull next time.* I took a deep breath and blew it out. *If at first you don't succeed...* I slid back into the car and pulled the other lever, and the trunk lid rose up. I smiled to myself. I scurried around behind the car, ready to tuck the beach towel back inside the trunk and get out of there. The contents of the trunk lay in full view now. A strong odor assaulted my nose. *Ugh! Men can be such slobs!*

Two white sketchpads and a stack of maps cluttered the floor of the trunk. A roll of electrical tape and a few short, thin ropes lay in the corner. In the middle of the trunk lay a long, bulging, dark duffle bag, and the striped towel that had spilled out of the closed trunk hung half in and half out of the duffle bag. *This bag must be his beach clothes.* I unzipped the bag and started to stuff the towel back into it when I noticed the towel had dried clumps of blood and hair on it. The inside of the bag stunk worse than the rest of the trunk. Instead of beach clothes though, I found a pair of khaki pants splattered with blood and a stack of sketches of girls about my age.

It was the drawing on top of the pile that sent a jolt through my body. I recognized the face as that of the girl in the newspaper. She wore a wild-eyed ghost-like stare, unlike the smiling picture of the girl in the newspaper, but there was no mistaking her for the same person. Attached to the sketch with a piece of Scotch tape was a green hair ribbon with *Barbara* stitched into it. I rifled through the other sketches. There was something very eerie about the other sketches, too. There were four in all and some of them had their eyes closed. All of them held their heads in unusual positions, and none of the girls smiled. Each of the sketches had something taped to the front, a locket, a charm, a ruffled sock, a barrette.

My stomach tightened, and the pulse in my throat traveled up my ears. I wanted to run. I needed to throw up. *Darlene! Where's Darlene? I need to warn her before I'm too late!* I closed the trunk and crept down the path closer to the clearing where Darlene was supposed to meet Stan. I reached the clearing. No Stan. No Darlene. Where were they?

The area was still laid out for a picnic. A basket and a thermos, and a few pieces of tinfoil lay across a green-striped blanket. Where could they have gone? A couple of cigarette butts and a half empty vodka bottle littered a nearby tree stump. A rock prevented a piece of paper from blowing away. It was a sketch of Darlene. She had a sad expression in her eyes. Her mouth was turned down in a pout and large dark smears of mascara dribbled down her cheeks. Her full breasts spilled over the top of my halter top. There was a thick dark "X" marked across the drawing.

Suddenly, I heard heavy footsteps moving toward me from the far path. I ran for cover into some thick bushes and held my breath as I peered out through the leaves. It was Stan, and he was alone. He quickly scoured the clearing, cleaning everything up. He shoved the tinfoil and Thermos into the basket. Then he walked over to the tree trunk, picked up the cigarette butts and poured the remaining vodka out onto the ground, shoving the bottle into the basket. He picked up the sketch, crushed it in one hand, and slammed the rock against the tree trunk just before he headed up the path toward the car.

I waited to give him time to leave. I heard the trunk being opened and closed shut. It would be just a few more seconds and the car door should slam and the engine would start, but nothing happened. Instead, I heard shuffling and Stan curse. I heard his heavy step coming back down the path. What had he forgotten? I peered out through the bushes one more time. There he stood in the clearing, holding fast to my roller skates. He held them in front of him with one hand. In the other hand he carried the tape and ropes.

"I know you're out there, sweetie," he sang in a deep, smooth voice. "I know you wouldn't leave your skates behind. And I know you've been snooping in my trunk. It's not nice to spy on people, Bibi. Why don't you just come out and we'll talk about things... boyfriend to girlfriend...okay? I'll set up the picnic for us again, and we'll enjoy the rest of the day now that my session with Darlene is over."

Through the branches, I saw him drop the skates, tape, and rope near the tree stump. He began circling the area, pushing branches aside. His voice rose a little and became more demanding. "Come on now, game over. I need to talk to my girl."

I stayed put, watching his every move as he continued to scour the area. I felt like a trapped animal. My heart thumped through my chest and up into my throat. I started to feel dizzy and weak. My legs grew rubbery.

He came closer and closer to where I was hiding, pulling back branches and plowing through brush. My ears buzzed and a wave of nausea coursed through me. I concentrated on my breathing, shallow and quiet. My body started to twitch and tremble and I felt I was going to wet my pants. I squeezed my legs to keep them still. Stan stood only about three feet from me when he suddenly let out a tremendous roar. "Come out now, you little bitch!"

The angry sound of his voice jolted me. I shut my eyes, crouched down and started to pray, hot tears streaming down my cheeks. Then it happened. I hiccupped. I opened my eyes to look around, certain he had heard me. I slapped my hand across my mouth and squeezed my nose. Another stifled hiccup escaped.

Through the bushes I watched Stan stop suddenly and posture like an animal on high alert. I tried holding my breath. It didn't work. I gasped for air and another hiccup burst forth. He stared straight at the clump of bushes I was hiding in and slowly and deliberately crept toward me.

"I know you're in there. Come out and we'll have a picnic." His voice sounded soft and syrupy now as if he were coaxing an animal into a snare.

The jig was up. I jumped out of the bushes, screamed for help, and ran for my life, back in the direction of Stan's car, trying to reach the road where I figured I'd be safe. He wouldn't dare do anything in broad daylight. I would be too close to houses. I barged through brush and brambles, thorns gouging my arms and legs and scratching my face. I heard him charging through the brush after me. I was almost to the road, gasping and hiccupping and crying. My bladder let loose and wet warmth trickled down the inside of my thighs. My legs felt hot and twitchy. Suddenly, the noise of his pursuit stopped. I had lost him, or he had given up chasing me.

I'm getting away! I'm getting away! In a few short yards I'll be free. Blood roared through my head and I felt dizzy with relief. *I'm almost there!*

And suddenly, as if out of nowhere, there he stood. His arms crossed in front of him, his body blocking the path. "And where do you think you're going?"

CHAPTER 19

I screamed at the top of my lungs. Stan lunged at me and clamped one rough hand over my mouth and grabbed my hair and yanked with the other. He dragged me, kicking and squirming, down the path and back into the clearing. He headed for the tree stump and sat down, bending my body into submission, and forced me into a sitting position on his lap. I continued to kick and squirm, clawing at his face. He let go of my hair and lay one arm across my chest and pinned my arms in front of me, and then braced one of his legs over my knees. Both my arms and legs were locked into place.

He pressed his cheek against mine and whispered hot, breathy words into my right ear. "I'm going to take my hand off your mouth now, and put it on your throat. If you as much as let out a peep, I will snap that pretty little neck of yours right now." Then he rolled his lips and flicked his tongue across my neck. I shivered.

"Remember, just one tiny peep and …snap!"

I shut up. Stan slowly removed his hand from my mouth and placed it firmly around my throat. I gasped for air.

"Ah," he smiled. "That's better. I can feel that little heart of yours beating. Is it beating that quickly for me? I think so. I think you like me."

I could feel my heart thumping out a war dance in my throat. I tasted sour bile and swallowed.

"Let's just sit here for a while and calm down." Stan relaxed his hold on my arms and legs and started to stroke my hair. "Let me fix your pretty hair. After all, I want it to be perfectly in place when I sketch you. While I'm fixing your hair, you can tell me what you saw and heard when you were playing detective."

I didn't speak.

"Oh yes. You are an obedient, sweet girl. You may talk now." He relaxed his grip around my throat.

"I didn't see or hear anything."

His hand angrily gripped my throat. "Don't lie to me. You're an honest girl. Honest girls don't lie. Now tell me."

Hot tears gushed down my cheeks and ran down my nose. "Please don't kill me. I won't tell anyone about anything. I can keep a secret."

"It's true, you have been very good about keeping secrets so far. I can't believe you didn't tell anyone about our little spin around town. You didn't tell anyone about our golf lesson, or the fact that we were going to meet for a sketching session. I know your father and mother never suspected a thing. You didn't tell anyone else, did you? Did you?" he growled.

"No, Stan, it was our secret. I'm good at keeping secrets, and I can keep this one, too. Just let me go and I'll prove it."

He relaxed his hand on my throat again and smiled a lunatic kind of smile, his eyes wide and vacant. He stood up and gently sat me back on the tree stump. He picked up the rope and tape and knelt down in front of me.

140

I closed my eyes tight and bit my lip. *This is it. I'm going to die.*

He ripped off a large piece of tape and covered my mouth, and then he pulled me over to a nearby tree and forced me to hug the trunk. He then tied my wrists together in front of me.

"I'm sorry to have to do this, but I have my sketch pad and charcoals in the car, and I want you here when I return. Sit tight for just a little while," he said very matter-of-factly. Then he smiled and winked at me and walked off down the path to his car.

I heard him open his trunk and slam it shut. Then I heard the engine of another car pull up.

"Good afternoon, officer," came Stan's calm voice.

A policeman! I'm going to be saved! I tried screaming as loud as I could, but the tape strained against my mouth, and all that came out were tiny mouse-like squeaks. I shimmied my arms up the tree trunk and stood up. I scraped my taped mouth across the rough tree bark, trying desperately to pry off the tape, while I struggled to free my hands from the tight ropes. I kicked the dirt to make noise and attract the policeman's attention.

"Hello. Got car trouble?" the policeman asked.

"No. Just thought I'd do some sketching. I heard there was a nice clearing back here. Home on leave, ya know. No time for this luxury when I'm on duty."

"A soldier, are you?"

"Yes sir! Private First-Class Polansky, United States Army at your service. Here's my ID." I envisioned him saluting. There was a pause while I guessed that the policeman checked his ID.

I kicked and screamed, even banged my head against the tree trunk to try to emit any sound that would carry. Nothing was loud enough. I spotted my skates behind me, a short distance away. *If I could just stretch far enough, I might be able to snag one with my leg and kick it forward into the path close enough for the policeman to hear it.*

I scraped my wrists hard against the trunk, and I kicked the tree trunk with all my might, but my rubber soles didn't create any sound. Stretch…stretch…The tip of my shoe could barely reach the closest skate. The husky sounds of male conversation and joking floated across the bushes. The policeman told Stan about his cousin who had enlisted right out of high school.

I strained and twisted my leg as far as I could, hooking the skate with my toe, and then swung my leg to ram the skate up the path. I heard it clunk into the bushes. The conversation stopped. *Success! Come and get me! Get me out of here!*

Then I heard the policeman chuckle. "Be careful of critters around here. Sounds like one's hiding in those bushes over there."

"Yes sir. Actually, critters are great to sketch. I especially like the wild ones."

The policeman chuckled again. "Okay. I guess I'll be on my way, Private First-Class Polansky. And thank you for serving our country. I salute you, sir."

"Thank you, officer. Nice talking to you."

I heard the police car drive away and my heart sank.

A minute later Stan loped back down the path whistling. His footsteps and whistling stopped for a couple of seconds, and I heard him curse, and then he started to whistle again. He arrived in the clearing holding my roller skate in one hand and his sketching materials in the other.

He laid the sketch pad and charcoals down on the ground next to the tree stump, and he stood in front of me, swinging the skate back and forth by its strap in front of my face. He shook his head as a father would to a disobedient child. His eyes clouded over.

"I told you to be good, and it was naughty of you to try to get that policeman's attention. Fortunately, he was too stupid to notice anything. But Officer Stupid is gone now, and it's just you and me now." He sneered at me under hooded eyes.

I trembled and my eyes twitched. I pressed my face into the tree and shut my eyes. Hot tears dripped down my cheeks.

"Oh, sweetie, don't turn away. Your sketching session is about to begin. Now I never sketch my victims...oops...I mean models, tied to a tree with tape on their mouths. There's nothing artistic about that. I need to untie you and take this tape off, but I need to know you won't scream because if you do, that will have to be the end of our session. Can I trust you?"

I didn't move.

"Can I trust you, I said!" He grabbed my collar.

I kept my face turned toward the tree and nodded my head.

"Good. That's what I was hoping. So, I don't think we'll need this anymore." He tore off the tape and kissed me on the mouth. "Such a sweet little mouth. Sorry I had to make it red." He touched my cheek.

I turned away.

"Shy all of a sudden?" He untied my hands. He tossed the rope and tape off out of view.

"Now sit right here for a minute." He led me back to the tree stump. "I have a surprise for you." He reached into his pocket and pulled out Darlene's locket. My eyes stared at the necklace.

"Darlene left this behind. We both agreed it looks prettier on you."

Stan drew a knife out of his pocket and slowly walked toward me. I tried to scream and nothing came out but a pathetic whimper.

"Please don't kill me. I'll be good."

As he placed the cold blade to my neck, I shut my eyes tight and clenched my jaw and neck muscles, preparing for the inevitable. He tugged at the twine necklace and cut it off my neck. My roller skate key tumbled to the ground. He then slipped behind me and fastened the locket onto my neck.

"I like all of my models to wear something pretty for their sessions. There." He ran his fingers across my neck. He stepped back and stared at me. "Oh, you look so pretty." Then he reached his hands down and squeezed his crotch.

I started to gag and threw up.

"What's the matter with you! Now, you've made a mess. Clean yourself up!" He handed me his handkerchief. I thought back to the last time he had let me use his handkerchief and how good it smelled and how I had wanted to keep it forever. I swiped the cloth across my mouth, spit into the dirt, and wiped again. I handed it back to him.

"Get that dirty rag away from me! You've wrecked the mood, you dirty girl. Throw it over there into those bushes."

I hurled the handkerchief into the bushes. Suddenly, mustering a little courage, I asked, "What did you do to Darlene?"

"Oh yeah, your little friend? She's a slut and she disgusts me. She was made up and dressed like a whore. I sent her home. She'll have a headache in the morning from all my *special* lemonade and she'll have a good cry for herself because I don't like her. Now, you...you're more my type. See you really trusted me and set up your appointment with me for the right reasons. You actually thought we were going to surprise your mommy and daddy. How sweet is that? I like sweet, Bibi. All the drawings of the girls in my car... yes... I know you found them... were of sweet girls...very sweet."

"If you really let Darlene go, she'll tell on you!" I blurted out.

"Oooh. Darlene's going to tell on me. I'm sooo scared. What is she going to say? That she made herself up, put on slutty clothes, lied to her mother, and got drunk in the woods with an older man who sent her home because he couldn't stand the sight of her? No, she's not going to say anything to anyone. She's probably passed out across her bed right now, sleeping off her first drunk."

I gritted my teeth and swallowed the bile that rose in my throat. "What are you going to do to me?"

"I'm going to sketch you, honey, in that pretty little locket you were wearing the night of your parents' party. But, do you know what else I think I'll have you wear? I think I'll have you put on your skates." He picked up the skates and placed them in front of me. "I love the way your legs look in them. I'll watch as you put them on. You can get started now." He squeezed his crotch again. He stared at me, his eyes wild and wide as I fumbled to put on the skates.

I didn't want to put them on. I knew that I couldn't easily run away from him in the woods if I was on skates. Putting them on would seal my fate. I pretended to struggle with the straps, unable to figure out how to put them on.

"Hurry up! You're taking too long!" he bellowed.

"I, I can't do it. I'm too jittery. And I think I'm going to be sick again. I can't," I whined. I turned away and pretended to gag.

His face contorted in anger. He grabbed my hair and yanked my face up close to his. "Do not get sick, you little bitch. Those skates are going on your feet if I have to put them on you myself." He picked up the first skate and yanked my foot and raised it in front of me. He started to force the toe of my shoe into the metal clamps of the skate. This was my only chance. I pulled my foot back and slammed it against his nose as hard as I could. He staggered, holding his nose, and the skate dropped in front of me. I knew I only had a second before he recovered. I picked up the skate and grabbed the leather strap and swung it with all my might at the side of his face, smashing him across the temple. Crack! The skate hit metal on bone like the blast of a heavy rock, and Stan staggered and fell. Blood spilled from his head and he lay still at my feet.

I killed him! I killed him! I'm a murderer!

I stood over him, my heart racing, my stomach turning. I screamed and screamed. "He's dead! He's dead! I killed him." I sobbed and stood over his body. I wanted to run away, to wake up out of this awful nightmare.

"Why did you make me do this? Why did you make me hurt you?" I stared at him.

I couldn't go home and tell my parents I had just murdered him. They liked Stan. *I'm going to prison! Do they put kids in prison?*

I stared at his lifeless body, an expression of shock on his face. I ran to the bushes to throw up again and collapsed on the ground, my hands over my face. The blood on Stan's head stopped seeping out and started to turn brown.

Stan's dead. The whole army will be after me. I can't face my family. What will Nancy and her family think? It's all over for me. I have to make a run for it. If I can get out onto the street my skates will carry me faster and farther away from here than on foot.

I picked up the bloody skate and realized I was holding the murder weapon. I searched for the other one and spotted it just to the right of Stan's shoulder. Just as I reached across his body to get it, Stan raised his hand, grabbed my hair, and pulled me to my knees.

"You heartless little bitch! You were going to leave me here to die! You were going to take off on your stupid roller skates and leave me here to die!" His face contorted, veins popping in his neck, and his eyes became wide and wild again. He grabbed my throat and started to press against my windpipe. "You had to wreck everything!"

I clenched my jaw to keep my neck from collapsing under the pressure of his fingers. I struggled with all my strength to pry his hands from my neck. I scratched at his eyes, and one of his hands loosened and he struck me hard across my face. I fell back and started to kick and scream with all my might. My head felt like it was going to burst.

He lunged at me and threw his body on top of me. He grabbed my neck with both hands and started to squeeze again. "I'm going to snap your pathetic little neck just like I did for the rest of my fan club!" He let out a maniacal laugh. "They deserved …"

Click. "Let go of that girl, or you'll be singin' high soprano very soon."

There stood Old Lady Brown, her gray curls peeking over the barrel of a real live gun aimed at Stan's crotch. I guess Jimmy Springer wasn't lying after all.

Stan released his grip and shot away from me. I stood in slow motion, all wabbly-like, gulping and gasping for air.

"Listen lady, don't do anything you'll be sorry for," Stan said as he slowly inched toward the old woman.

"Come any closer and I'll shoot."

Stan stopped. "You wouldn't want to hurt a soldier in the United States Army, would you?"

"I don't care if you're the commander-in-chief, himself. I'll shoot it off if you come any closer. I told that cop something fishy was going on here," she said. "He thinks I'm just an old bag who's losing my marbles." The old woman looked at me. "What's your name, girly?"

"Bibi Reilly," I choked out.

"You okay? 'Cause if not, you just tell me and I'll shoot this character."

"I'm okay," I gulped. It hurt to swallow. It hurt to breathe.

"You live around here, don't you?"

"Yes, ma'am."

"Me and Josephine here," she patted her gun, "we're gonna keep a close eye on this snake while you run on home and have your mama call the cops. Tell them to come real quick 'cause I don't know how long I'll be able to control Josephine."

"Yes, ma'am." I turned and ran down the path and headed out of the street. Before I even cleared the woods, I heard one loud shotgun blast. I guessed that was Old Lady Brown shooting his you-know-what off.

The sound of the blast flushed everyone in the neighborhood out into the street. By the time I got to my house, Mom and Aunt Addie and the twins were all standing in the front yard looking around. My aunt was yelling to Mr. Traski that she wasn't going to any bomb shelter. I ran into my mother's arms, sobbing. Snot ran down my nose and puke dribbled over my lips, while my body quaked and shivered. My legs twitched. My words were jumbled and garbled, my voice raspy and deep. I didn't even sound like myself. I guess I got enough information out because I saw Aunt Addie go to the phone and call the police. That's the last thing I remember before I blacked out.

***

I awoke to the sounds of sirens and Mom's voice calling my name. I suddenly remembered where I was and what had happened, and I was sure the police were here to arrest me for attempted murder. My mother's anxious face hovered over me, and next to her, holding tight to Josephine, was Old Lady Brown.

"Did you… you know…shoot it off?"

"Naw. Not that he didn't deserve it. I just wanted him to know I meant business."

I gave her a weak smile. "Thanks, Mrs. Brown."

"Well, I'll take Josephine home now. You get some rest before those cops come over and want to talk with you." Then she bent down and whispered in my ear. "I hope they hang the creep."

The Final Chapter

The police came out to get my story early that evening, and they assured me I was not going to be arrested. They congratulated me for being such a quick thinker and said I was lucky. Somehow, I didn't feel all that lucky. They paid a visit to Mrs. Brown. I heard she let them have it for not believing her the first time she called. The police roped off the woods until they finished their investigation and they towed Stan's car away. My roller skates were taken as evidence.

The police visited Darlene's house that same night.

The next day she and her mother left to visit her grandmother in White Plains for a few weeks. Stan had been right about one thing—Darlene never did speak to me about what happened in the woods that afternoon.

A week after Stan's arrest, a FOR SALE sign went up on the Polanskys' front lawn. Nancy broke down and told her parents that Stan had been molesting her for the past two summers. He threatened to tell all her friends about it unless she kept "their little secret." She spends most of her time indoors now, except for her weekly trips to a psychiatrist.

Aunt Addie headed back to California as soon as my father got his license reinstated. She attends Alcoholic Anonymous meetings a couple times a week while she works at keeping sober. She calls often. Her business picked up tremendously, now that her customers can depend on her opening up regularly.

As for me, the next couple of weeks were a blur. I stayed close to home and answered a lot of questions. All of my summer secrets spilled out. I spent time thinking about what a close call I had and wondering how I could have been so wrong about Stan.

Danny returned from his fishing trip and I told him all about Henry. He was relieved that Henry had finally taken his first flight. I tried to make the story as dramatic as I could. I'm a pretty good storyteller. Danny listened and said he would hire me anytime and that maybe someday we'd both be veterinarians. It was good talking about something normal again.

As days passed, I realized my conscience grew lighter and I felt younger, more like myself. And I didn't mind being just thirteen one bit.

For the rest of the summer, radios and newspapers released new information about the case. Mom and Dad turned off the radio when I entered the room, and they threw out newspapers as soon as they read them.

I remember the chill I felt when I emptied the garbage a couple days after my close call and saw Stan's face and the pictures of four young smiling girls, all about my age, staring at me from the front page of the *Stamford Advocate*. I fished the paper out of the garbage and wiped spaghetti sauce off of it.

SERIAL KILLER CAPTURED (Springdale)

After eighteen months and four brutal rapes and killings, the police took Stanley Polansky, 22, into custody on Tuesday. Private First-Class Polansky was dishonorably discharged from the army two years ago for behavior unbefitting a United States soldier. Police say the handsome soldier, a dropout of Worcester Art School, charmed young girls into meeting him to be sketched, and then raped them and broke their necks, morbidly drawing their portraits after death. On Tuesday, Stanley Polansky's luck ran out when his intended victim, a thirteen-year-old Springdale girl, narrowly escaped and was able to identify him. Incriminating evidence was found in Mr. Polansky's car, linking him to all four deaths. Polansky is being held without bail until his arraignment.

I stared at the article and tried to remember the good Stan who had helped my aunt, the fun Stan who played golf with my father and drove him to work, the considerate Stan who brought flowers to brighten my mother's day, and the charming Stan who had stolen my heart. Instead, the face that stared back at me from the newspaper was that of a dangerous, manipulative stranger who may not have succeeded in killing me, but would always be able to claim me as one of his victims.

The End

The Author Speaks to Teens

Although this story reads like a memoir, and there really is a Springdale, Connecticut, the story is purely a work of fiction. It deals with sensitive subjects and fragile individuals. It's not meant to shock, but instead to inform.

Alcoholism and sexual abuse ruin lives. In the story you just read, Bibi Reilly was an innocent victim of both. Her Aunt Addie had a drinking problem and Stan was a charming, yet dangerous, sexual predator.

Unlike a young child, a teenager will often sense that things aren't right or normal, and yet struggle to define what's wrong. Often, they won't speak to a trusted adult about it. Instead they'll ignore the problem and hope it will just go away. It doesn't.

I wrote this book after I learned that a close friend of mine had been sexually molested as a child. I was shocked and troubled for a long time, so I began studying about sexual predators and how they insipidly creep into our lives. I learned they are not always the stranger on the street who pulls up next to you in a non-descript van offering candy, who prompts you to run down the street yelling "Stranger danger!"

More commonly, the predator is someone you know—adults who would rather spend time with you than hang out with people their own age. And when they earn your trust, they make their move. They "groom" their victims and often prey on troubled and naïve youths, or the child of a family in crisis. As in the story, they convince you to agree to "keep it secret."

As for alcoholism, I learned about that firsthand by living with an alcoholic for fifteen years. Many of my days and nights were spent covering up my embarrassment and making excuses for his behavior. My social life, my self-esteem, and my soul suffered. I was no match for this ruthless disease, so I walked away from the marriage.

Do you suspect that someone close to you has a drinking problem? Alateen is a peer support group for teenagers who are struggling with the effects of another's drinking problem. To find a location and meeting times in your area, check out this website: https://al-anon.org/al-anon-meetings/find-an-alateen-meeting/ If you wish to learn more statistics about alcoholism, visit the website: https://www.learn-about-alcoholism.com/statistics-on-alcoholics.html

Are you uncomfortable with the inappropriate sexual way someone speaks to you or touches you? If so, the first thing to do to get it to stop is to tell an adult whom you trust. There is a phone number both of you can call, and what you tell the counselor who answers the phone will be held confidential. You don't even need to give your name. That number is 800.656. HOPE, or check out this website: http//www.online.rainn.org. According to The Joyful Heart Foundation, which researches sexual violence, 1 in 3 females are victims of sexual assault, while 1 in 6 males are victims. Those are very high statistics.

Is there someone in your life whom you like a lot, who compliments you and then belittles you, making you feel special one day and worthless the next like Stan did to Bibi? This is a pattern that abusers use to manipulate and control their victims. It forms a toxic relationship.

It's important to know that there are young people who face these issues every day, and that there is help available. Learn the signs and keep yourself from becoming a victim.

J. S.

Acknowledgements

It has been said that writing is a lonely occupation. I disagree. To do it correctly, I believe you need to surround yourself with smart, caring and supportive individuals—lots of them—people who stand by you unconditionally, giving of their precious time to read something once more, to share one more insight, or to render one more great suggestion. I am blessed to have people like this in my life, more accomplished, more prolific, more successful than I. They are the Wallingford Women's Writers, Pamlico Writers' Group, and Coastal Carolina Kid Lit Group. I am forever grateful for your confidence in me.

Many thanks to my editors, Rose Green, Mary Kacillas, and Susann Camus whose keen eyes helped me polish this story and craft it into something of which I am proud.

Thank you to my beta readers extraordinaire—Peggy Coe Campbell, Colleen Serreno, and Patricia Maury. Your questions and insights were invaluable in helping me pinpoint and revise the story's weaknesses before sending it out into the world. I love you all.

I need to extend special thanks to award-winning children's author Mary Sharnick who was generous to read and review my book and lend an extraordinary quote for its cover.

And finally, all my love and thanks to my husband and alpha reader, Larry, who spent many days and evenings alone while I sat in my study at my computer completely engrossed in Bibi Reilly's world. You are the best!

~ J. S.